By Land, by Sea

Other Fiction by William Hoffman

The Trumpet Unblown (1955)
Days in the Yellow Leaf (1958)
A Place for My Head (1960)
The Dark Mountains (1963)
Yancey's War (1966)
A Walk to the River (1970)
A Death of Dreams (1973)
Virginia Reels (1978)
The Land That Drank the Rain (1982)
Godfires (1985)

STORIES BY

William Hoffman

by land, by sea

Louisiana State University Press
Baton Rouge   1988

Copyright © 1978, 1980, 1982, 1984, 1985, 1986, 1987, 1988 by William Hoffman
All rights reserved
Manufactured in the United States of America

Designer: Laura Roubique Gleason
Typeface: Aldus
Typesetter: The Composing Room of Michigan
Printer: Thomson-Shore, Inc.
Binder: John H. Dekker & Sons, Inc.

10 9 8 7 6 5 4 3 2

The author gratefully acknowledges the editors of *Atlantic Monthly, McCall's, Sewanee Review,* and *Virginia Quarterly Review,* in which some of these stories previously appeared.

Library of Congress Cataloging-in-Publication Data

Hoffman, William, 1925–
    By land, by sea.

    I. Title.
PS3558.034638B9   1988   813'.54   87-21381
ISBN 0-8071-1390-5

Publication of this book has been supported by a grant from the National Endowment for the Arts in Washington, D.C., a federal agency.

The paper in this book meets the guidelines for performance and durability of the Committee on Production Guidelines for Book Longevity of the Council on Library Resources.∞

For Diana and Josiah Bunting

contents

By Land, by Sea

fathers and daughters

Youngsters who attended the private school, the academy, had a word for the boy's kind: grit. Negroes, blacks, went to the consolidated public school in Virginia's rural King Charles County, and a few whites, sons and daughters of parents who no longer thought of themselves as white or as anything except cornered.

Ruth, Cortney's daughter, brought the "grit" home in early spring. She was a trim, quick girl whose off-blond hair had been clipped short, yet bounded with her energy. Her skin tanned easily, and she'd already spread her beach towel just outside her second-story window on the porch roof of the white farmhouse. Her radio rippled alien music across freshening pastures to the pond, where cattle lifted mystified heads.

The grit was Richard Talin, a savagely handsome boy whose bones punched into skin of his olive face. He wore his black hair uncut, Indian fashion, and his dark eyes were wild, those of an animal fearful of being tricked into a cage. He had on leather sandals, jeans, and a sleeveless athletic shirt—an orange 7 against black nylon. Walking, he hooked thumbs over his hip pockets and worked his elbows like wings.

"Richard's the slugging ace of the baseball team," Ruth said, as if exhibiting a prime young bull. She held to the link formed by one of his bare, muscled arms.

Cortney kept thinking of his daughter that way—holding on to the boy's arm. Next day, as he moved through his lumberyard in Tobaccoton, Cortney glimpsed Wayne LeSeur standing among immaculate ricks of newly sawn pine. Wayne coached the academy baseball team. Cortney asked what kind of player Richard was.

"Don't know," Wayne said. His tongue prodded the chaw in his lustrous cheek. "No Rebel he."

"You mean the boy's at the county school?"

"If he's in any school a-tall. My experience is the Talins is rowdydowdies."

Cortney spoke with his wife, Dottie. She knelt before the wraparound porch, where she was planting a border of scarlet sage. She stopped pushing the trowel into loam and dabbed at her forehead with the back of a wrist.

"Why, however did she meet him?" Dottie asked.

"The white boys from the county school hang around the academy. Wayne says Richard Talin comes each afternoon to watch her on the tennis court."

"He is a pretty thing, but I expect Ruth's just collecting scalps."

Collecting scalps, the game girls played of luring boys into romantic traps. Ruth was a junior at the academy. During her three years of upper school, she'd hung a dozen of those scalps from the oval mirror of her dressing table—evidenced by photographs, bits of ribbon and lace, faded nosegays.

Cortney felt relieved, sure that he would soon again see sons of men he knew, people whose predictability he understood.

Yet it seemed to be only Richard. The rawboned boy waved, grinned, and tossed his coarse hair. He owned a car, a Corvair, with fenders missing, jumbo tires, and an engine that sounded mighty enough to power a bulldozer. When Richard drove onto the lane from the highway, he never slowed but shot up swirling dust behind him as if red soil were his banner.

He couldn't swim. He didn't possess a bathing suit and slid into Cortney's blue pool the first time wearing cutoff jeans. Ruth teased and egged him on. Richard's black chest hair curled against his tinted skin like ringlets. Even wet, he didn't appear altogether clean.

Ruth held her palms upward beneath his body and coaxed him into stroking. After a few days he could paddle around the pool, always staying close to the safety ledge. Ruth, wearing her shocking-pink two-piece suit, put on a diving show, her small body tidy and precise. She was a girl, yet woman, the beginnings of a woman. Cortney hated the transformation.

Richard didn't know how to ride a horse. Oh, he could stay on, his hands gripping the mane like an attacking Apache. He whooped and hollered as they cantered across the pasture. The English saddle was foreign to him, and he called out, "Where's the steering wheel on this here ve-*hicle?*"

Cortney would look from his sawmill window to see them driving around Tobaccoton in Richard's smelly, scuttling Corvair. Or when Cortney went home for lunch, the shirtless boy might be sitting on the porch leafing through a magazine, drinking soda, and munching a sandwich. Ruth kept him fed.

"Doesn't he ever work?" Cortney asked when she padded past him from the kitchen. On a tray she carried pecan pie and cold milk.

"That boy's a wizard with a chain saw," she answered. She glanced toward the porch. "Daddy, he's nice."

"You all spending his money or yours?"

"My father, the original crab," she said. She puffed her cheeks and bugged her eyes at him before gliding away, holding the food as if it were a consecrated offering.

Cortney encountered Richard's father on a July morning when heat licked the skin with the flaying roughness of a cat's tongue. As Cortney drove his pickup among fields of parched, stunted corn, a mob of hogs charged toward him over sticky asphalt. They were a mottled, loutish, mud-crusted multitude, all squealing, bucking, and fleeing.

Farther on, a smashed truck lay on its side among dusty weeds of a drainage ditch. An unshaved, violent man whose denim shirt was black with sweat stood on the road shouting curses. He raved and ran after the hogs. In his fury, he stooped and snatched up rocks to hurl at them.

His name was lettered on the tilted truck cab, an uneven job in white paint—Parrish Donny Talin. The senior county deputy, Henry Thorpe, confirmed that the thrashing, howling figure was Richard's father. Henry said the family lived in a trailer just past the birch sloughs.

The brown trailer was propped on cinder blocks among scrub pines at the end of a rutted dirt road. Around the trailer were broomstraw and gutted car hulks. A brawny woman waddled down from the doorway. She wore a dress that hardly reached her knees. Her bare feet raised spouts of dust. Her black hair was wrapped around blue plastic curlers. On a hip she toted a laundry tub. As she hung wash, she stared at Cortney, who waved, yanked the pickup into gear, and headed home.

Dottie was sitting on the screened porch off the kitchen, snapping pole beans into a dip of white apron across her lap. He told her about driving out to the trailer, about the way the Talins lived. She knew what he was thinking.

"Poor whites," she said.

"Or worse. Ruth's beginning to talk like him."

"Half the county talks like him."

"Not our half."

"I can't believe she's deathly serious about the boy."

"He's around here so much I'm going to charge him room rent."

Richard kept Ruth out late at night. When Cortney asked where they went, she wasn't so much evasive as vague. Maybe she didn't know altogether. She and the boy moved in their own atmosphere, a couple floating through a sunny terrain that had no boundaries or exactness.

Cortney didn't become really upset till he suspected drinking. He'd lain in bed every night when the popping, snorting Corvair sped in and parked under the white oak. He'd heard music and giggling. Sunday morning, as he drove Dottie to the Presbyterian church, he saw that the glint on his brick gatepost at the end of the lane was an empty green bottle.

It was a wine bottle whose label read "Happy Rain" and pictured a wickedly delirious Cupid showering under a cluster of dripping purple grapes. The bottle had a daisy stuck into it.

"It didn't have to be Richard," Ruth said, back at the house. She was drying her hair, holding a pistol-like blower above it.

"You're swearing to me it wasn't?"

"Daddy, a little wine for the stomach. You drink every night."

"We're not equals. In fact he's not anything."

"He's thinking about his career," she said. "The Navy—he's been to Lynchburg to talk with a recruiter."

Cortney became calm. The Navy would take Richard many a mile, and in another year Ruth should be at William and Mary with her eye cocked for college men.

•

No more wine bottles on the gatepost, but late during a rasping August night, when Cortney stood in his pajamas at the bedroom window to air heat from his sorely burning body and to wait for Ruth, he looked out over the pasture toward the pond. In the moon glaze he thought he saw her and Richard running and heard laughter. Among the horses she and the boy appeared to be racing, leaping, both of them slim and stripped to a silvery nakedness.

Cortney wasn't certain it was real nakedness or simply moon sheen coupled with shameful images skittering through his mind.

Hurriedly he tiptoed down the steps to the side door and out to the white plank fence separating the house from the pasture. He looked toward the glowing slope and the luminous pond, where bullfrogs wonked-wonked-wonked. If he'd seen Ruth and Richard at all, they were gone among the pale weeping willows. Only cattle moved in the night.

"Cortney?" Dottie called from the window.

"Just cooling the body," he answered. Sweating and panting, he walked into the house and climbed to the muggy sheet Dottie's fingers had smoothed. He thought of Ruth's tan, girlish body lying hot beneath the willow branches, that muscled, dark grit of a wild boy sprawled on top of her. Cortney sat up.

"What is it?" Dottie asked, also rising.

"Bad dream," he said.

Instead of speaking to Ruth at the house, he told her to come by his office in the lumberyard. Richard entered beside her. Cortney explained he wanted a private word with his daughter. Richard tossed his head to lay his black hair. He would be at the Mockingbird Café. The closing door muffled the shrill of the saws.

Ruth wore tennis shoes, white shorts, and a pink, sleeveless blouse through which her brassiere showed. Sweat beaded down of her face. Cortney stared as if he could push inside her skull to the secret region of her mind. She looked back from green eyes flecked with darkness, a gaze of patient waiting but not submission.

"Are you intimate with him?" Cortney asked.

"Daddy, you have no right to question me like this."

"I have the right because nobody loves you more than I do, and I won't allow you to waste your beautiful young life on a pretty piece of trash who's using you. I'll forgive anything but never stop trying to help you."

For a moment she appeared so openly innocent and capable of being hurt, like a fragile bloom. She touched the corner of an eye with a childish finger. He would've gone around his desk to hug her, yet before he moved, a firmness flowed back into her, a sly mulishness.

"You shouldn't call people trash just because they don't talk the way we do or have as much money."

"I can't stop you from seeing him, but I'll not allow intimacy. Understand what I mean?"

She sat tensed, her small hands flat on her lap, her eyes lowered. Her lips trembled. She lifted moist eyes but still didn't speak. He kept his expression mean. When at last he nodded, she stood and escaped.

The talk did little if any good. The boy still came to the house, put up his feet, and threw cigarette butts on the sere lawn, causing grass to smolder. He often drove Ruth's yellow Mustang. When a fender was dented, Cortney didn't ask who'd been behind the wheel. He permitted his insurance company to pay for repairs.

August brought no rain. The wounded ground split, and tree shade was as thin as sunlight passed through a wafer.

Late Sunday, after everyone was in bed, one of the few nights Ruth hadn't been out with him, Richard slewed his outrageous car with its howling, hateful engine to the front of the house, where he honked his horn.

Furious, Cortney ran barefooted out the door. He wore only his pajama bottoms. The car's interior light was switched on, and the tape deck pounded with barbaric yapping. Richard himself held a Jew's harp to his loose mouth and hunched as he whipped a palm against the twanger. He reared, laughing.

"Oh, man, the world's turning over with them pretty colored fireflies!"

"Daddy!" It was Ruth, running in her short nightgown. "Daddy, I'll handle it!"

"Here, little kitty, kitty, pussy—"

Cortney smacked him. The boy's head had been lolling toward the window, and the blow knocked him sideways. The Jew's harp struck the car's floor. Ruth cried out. Richard struggled and cursed. He pushed a leg and part of his twisting body from the car. Ruth blocked and tried to soothe him as one would a wild horse.

"Nobody, I mean nobody, can do that to me!" the boy shouted. He clawed from his jeans a knife with a glimmering stiletto blade. Cortney felt sick. He thought of the loaded Smith & Wesson .38 in his bureau drawer.

Somehow Ruth grabbed the boy's arm and knife. She cut her fingers. Her blood shocked Richard into quietness. She shoved him inside the car and slammed the door. Dottie pulled at Cortney.

The engine gunned, Ruth stepped back, and the Corvair raced away down the lane, its horn honking long and defiantly. Dottie hurried Ruth to the house to doctor her fingers. Cortney stood shaking and thinking he might have been defeated in front of his daughter.

He lifted the knife she'd dropped. He closed it, hurled it into the pasture's darkness, and leaned against a white oak, clutching the trunk. Inside the house, his women wept.

•

He didn't believe Richard would return, yet without actual evidence he suspected Ruth was still seeing her lover. Cortney said nothing for fear she might run off with the boy to God knew where.

On Labor Day afternoon Cortney sat on his screened porch reading Tobaccoton's weekly paper. He heard flies buzzing and the car, its engine quietly popping.

For once Richard had on a suit, a woolly black serge, the kind primitive Baptists and Pentecostalists wore to preaching summer and winter. His hair had been cut and wetted, the part as rigidly placed as if slashed. He didn't enter the yard but stood at the white fence.

"I come to tell you I'm sorry about how I acted," he said, his fingers curved over the fence. "I never meant to do it."

Cortney, holding the newspaper, had pushed open the screen door. Richard's throat worked. Angles of his face were burnished olive slabs.

"But you shouldn'ta hit me either," he said.

"No, I shouldn't have," Cortney said.

"Okay then," the boy said. He walked stiffly to his car, folded himself inside, and drove slowly away from under the shade.

Ruth again brought him to the house. They grained the horses and threw rocks into the pond. He drove her out at night. They went to the academy football game. As a birthday present Richard bought her a charm bracelet and a rose.

A yellow September Sunday she took him fishing at the pond. He carried several rods and a paper sack holding six-inch black plastic worms. When Richard tramped up the slope at dusk, his back was bowed under the weight of glossy, astonished bass dangling from his twine stringer.

Cortney was aghast at the indecent number—all sizes but mostly two pounders and less, which he always threw back. And he would never use black plastic worms for bait. That a person possessed no more feeling than to deceive a noble fish with rubbery underwater wigglers caused him to mope and become angry all over again.

He'd stocked the pond himself, and he loved his bass, their rampant courage, their fully committed attack. Bass held nothing back, and when he boated one and gently squeezed the soft, slippery coolness of the white belly, he felt he gripped spirit itself.

To be sporting, he used only topwater bait, his rod laying flies in limpid fall among the dusty lily pads, his skill in his wrist and the sense of warping line forming horizontally behind him. He never carried home a fish unless it was of bullying size. Instead, he tenderly loosened the hook and allowed the bass to flip itself down into green shadows, its valor intact.

He didn't speak when Richard used two hands to heave up and display his catch. A glance from Ruth stayed Cortney's tongue. The glance was as close as she'd come to pleading. He climbed to his bedroom and sat till he felt his control return.

He would've tolerated even the bass massacre except that the next afternoon a dog—a ribbed, tail-tucking, ragged-eared hound—caused Cortney to slow his pickup and look toward a honeysuckle patch beside the road. More dogs circled, emerald flies spiraled, and the loathsome fish rotted in sunlight.

Cortney kicked at the dogs. Even meat hunters might be justified by putting food on the table for hungry mouths, but to kill and waste life was as close to evil as he could understand. With a shovel from his truck, he buried the fish.

He also went to the sheriff, a county man named Queensberry, who sat in the courthouse basement, beyond the bars, the office windowless and dank even while the land thirsted. It was a clean room, dusted and swept daily, with no clutter of warrants or wanted posters.

"You, a prominent citizen, wanting me to bend the law?" Queensberry asked, his weight sitting easy, yet alert, his red brows lifted.

"I'm asking you to enforce the law. The boy drives like a demon out of hell. He carouses, brawls, and carries a knife big enough to hack off a bear's leg. He's been talking Navy. You could encourage it. I'm not asking anything illegal.''

''That's good 'cause you won't get it. He has to step over the line.''

The next Saturday Richard lost his driver's license. Racing two rowdies along a secondary road, he bounced off a concrete culvert, crashed his Corvair through barbed wire, and plowed up stalks of gaunt, desiccated corn. Though the car rolled twice, Richard was only bloodied.

Queensberry found an opened bottle of Happy Rain wine. Richard's charge was drunk and reckless driving. When Queensberry chanced to meet Cortney in the Mockingbird Café, the sheriff said, ''I didn't do it for you. I had to pull his ticket to keep him from killing himself—or somebody.''

•

Even wheelless, Richard continued coming to the house. He'd hitch a ride and walk up the lane, or phone Ruth to fetch him from town. They raked burgundy leaves into windrows and burned them. During a cold, wet November they sat side by side in front of the living-room fire and listened to her tapes.

The first of December he left for Norfolk and the Navy. Ruth drove him to the bus. In later weeks she stood at her window and looked out at the bare, sleet-battered oaks. She was first to reach the mail. Each time the phone rang her breathing stilled.

Other boys, all from the academy, knocked on her door. In the house her phonograph played. She attended dances and rode her mare through a snow. She was elected a Homecoming princess and dressed herself in a pale blue satin gown to pose on a flowered float. If she cried, she did it within her bedroom's privacy.

Her quietness grew. She seemed to be forever listening. Cortney caught her looking at him. He would be reading the newspaper or poking the fire and turn to find her green eyes watching. He saw no resentment, no ugliness. Rather, it was as if she'd set him on scales and were weighing him.

Mostly she remained in her room. He and Dottie tried to bring her back into the family, but she was removed. The music she cloaked herself with, the laughter among boys, were camouflage. Cortney longed to pass his hand over her like a faith healer and take her pain into himself.

He believed she would be better in the green surge of spring, when pollen misted and the sweet rains brought peepers to voice at the pond. She was still on the academy's tennis team and had been accepted at William and Mary. Cortney bought her a chestnut foal to mother and raise.

She responded to the foal, a filly that timidly nibbled the salt from her palms. She invited her class out to the pool for a party under the colored lanterns. The neat, towheaded captain of the football team danced her across the slate flagstones.

In the heat of a summer night Cortney again stood at his bedroom window and looked toward the pasture and willow-lapped pond. Tree toads throbbed, and flickers of lightning profiled massing clouds that slid over the moon. A wind was rising.

He frowned, stooped, and stared. He pressed his forehead against the copper screen. He was experiencing a vision of Ruth running, dancing, and leaping among the horses—she and Richard silvery naked in the disturbed, whitened night.

He knew it couldn't be true, yet he hurried to Ruth's room, opened the door, and tiptoed to her bed. She slept on her back, her hands crossed over her breasts, her face pale and composed. She hadn't taken off Richard's bracelet. A bar of light from the hall lay aslant her throat.

For an instant he feared her dead. He leaned an ear to her breathing. Straightening, he thought of superstitious old people from his childhood who believed the soul left the body while it slept. As he stood over her with his head bowed, he felt she wasn't in the room at all, but out in the night amid the blowing orchard grass and luminous corn—a dear, glistening shape rising and whirling as freely as the untamable wind.

landfall

Chris's wife was not immediately suspicious. They'd been at sea two days before she set her unsteady gaze on the sun's position and glanced at the rolled charts in pigeonholes above the folding navigator's table. Once he would never have been able to fool her, but the medicine caused drowsiness and even absence—as if she'd floated upward and away.

Wyndor was an 11.5-meter wooden sloop they'd owned seventeen years, built for them at Bristol, Rhode Island, by antique shipwrights who remembered the sea as a personality, not a geographical area or path of trade. The boat had teak decking, brass fittings, and a 6-foot keel filled with lead shot, which made her stiff as a pilgrim.

Wyndor was the last of three boats he'd owned, and this was to be the final cruise before he gave the vessel over to a yacht broker. Chris counted stages of his life through boats—the first, the 21-foot daysailer he purchased while courting Belle; the second, a 9-meter cutter with bowsprit, bought despite his failure to win the Massachusetts judgeship; and finally *Wyndor*, the craft they'd splurged for and hung their concluding dreams on.

This time Belle hadn't wanted to come, or, rather, she hadn't believed they could two-hand *Wyndor* any longer, though they'd twice sailed from Boston to the Bahamas and back, done it outside on the ocean rather than used the inland route to Florida and the dash from Lake Worth. Belle, hands in her lap, preferred sitting and watching sugar maples transform themselves into autumn fire. Sunlight moved over her in her chair before the window of their home like golden gauze being drawn across her body.

He talked her into it—just a week's cruise, he promised. With luck, Indian summer would hold. "We'll stay in close," he said. "A short trip toward Yarmouth, and we turn back the instant we tire."

The first morning a southwesterly breeze carried the overripe scent of land, and *Wyndor* ran, creating her quiet sibilance. Chris no longer set a spinnaker—the maneuver was too slippery and arduous—but he allowed the jenny to balloon, and the boat pitched forward languidly.

He watched the sky, listened to weather reports, and checked their position on the Loran. Belle had been a better navigator and even a few months ago would not have allowed him to take over the charts, but now her eyes misted and blurred when she did close work. Along the coast he shot bearings on a beacon, a church steeple, and a sunken freighter whose portholes gushed the rising tide.

They saw ships coming down from Canada, one a listing cargo carrier with a gashed bow. She flew a Greek flag. Chris waved, but nobody was on deck, and he didn't try to make radio contact. Sunlit gulls followed the ship, circling upward on its drafts.

During the afternoon while Belle slept, Chris changed course fifteen degrees eastward. When he heard her below, he brought the compass back to its original heading.

She climbed up the companionway and blinked toward the bow. He fixed flotation cushions for her in the cockpit. She rubbed her thin hands and breathed deeply of the sea smells. For a time she didn't notice but then turned westward. She leaned to the binnacle to read the compass card.

"I thought we were staying close in," she said.

"We can save a day by holding course," he said. That at least was true.

"I didn't know we had to save days any longer, and I don't feel like standing watches."

"I'm not sleepy. I'll set the vane and smoke my pipe."

She tired quickly, much more so than he, who no longer felt himself strong. What he felt was brittle. Occasionally, in removing his shoes, he glimpsed his deflated calves, their toadstool color. He tried not to see his body in the mirror after a shower. What had become of his shoulders?

Shoulders he had when he first saw Belle in a Newport boatyard. He was a Harvard law student, and she'd just hoisted herself by bos'n's chair up a yawl's mast. Her slim legs dangled from a candy-striped skirt, and her strong, tanned arms looped over her head as she examined couplings of the mast's jumper stays.

The second time he saw her was in a Boston College parade, she riding on a float of white gardenias shaped like a pirate ship. She stood dressed in a buccaneer's costume—black shorts, boots, a patch over one eye. She raised a toy cutlass.

He followed the parade to find her name and eventually fought her Irish boyfriend, he and the boyfriend bloodying each other on her dormitory lawn until they were too weary to continue throwing their arms.

Now Belle was diminishing, her flaxen hair having given way to wavy whiteness, her girlish body sunken and curved, her biceps hardly larger than her wrists. She couldn't weigh more than eighty pounds. Her bones had become twigs.

"Let's stay out another night," he said. "We have the moon, and I'd rather be up here than below."

"I don't like not standing my watches."

"I confess I snooze a little."

He knew the sounds and rhythms of *Wyndor* so well that when he set her course, the slightest variation in her motion or voice wakened him. Belle too would have once immediately sensed a change of direction, but now she slept the night and most of the day.

He attempted to block pictures from entering his mind, memories of her trim and fast, especially images of her diving. She'd been on the B.C. swim team, and her erect body stretched as muscled as a boy's as she gave herself from the board to the air—for an instant a sculpted sacrifice.

Stuffy she'd thought him. He'd been born of a family in which one grandfather was a Congregational minister and the other a Republican congressman. Without her Chris would have settled into a premature sedateness, an ossification of mind and spirit, but Belle made him ski and take dancing lessons, and shamed him into learning to fly a Piper Cub.

They were nearly flying now, averaging seven knots on a corrected course of sixty degrees. The moon was so bright that shadows of the mast, stays, and shrouds ran beside *Wyndor*. They saw more ships, some moving slowly at oblique angles, their running lights merging with stars on the purple horizon.

She insisted on standing a watch. He napped on his berth, ready to leap, and felt her touch through the boat. Her hands were no longer firm on the helm. When he went topside, she sat tilted among cushions, her chin declining, her fingers falling away from a steering spoke.

"I want to go in," she said.

"We'll never have a better run," he said. He heated sweet rolls and carried her a mug of coffee. The breeze, though still fresh and benign, had backed.

"I'm too old to fight a gale," she said.

"We're only a few miles offshore. I'll show you our position."

He brought up charts, and the position he penciled in was a false one south of Cape Sable. They were actually well out in the North Atlantic.

"We ought to see some land," she said.

"You're tired."

"Tiredness has nothing to do with what I see—or don't."

She fought to hide pain. She had surrendered to pills as if the taking of medicine were an evil given in to.

She possessed her father's resoluteness: he'd been a career Army man, an infantry colonel who died at Cologne during World War II. Belle herself had enlisted in the WACS, where she served as a chauffeur for Washington brass. Chris, a captain judge-advocate, had written her a V-mail every other day for the two years he was in the Pacific.

She couldn't stay awake. She used cushions to wedge her lean body into the cockpit and set her face to compass and course, but her eyelids drooped and her head sank. Wind lifted wisps of hair not protected by her blue kerchief. He sat beside her and laid his hand on hers.

"You're doing something," she said when she came up from her long afternoon nap.

"Think so?"

"I used the Loran. Do you intend to tell me where we're going?"

"Newfoundland. In this weather we can make St. John's—put in for a few days' rest and head back."

"Why did you deceive me?"

"I knew it was more than you'd agree to, and when this cruise ends, we lose *Wyndor*. I find that hard to accept."

"Nobody's forcing you to sell. The children will take her."

"They're not children but busy, middle-aged people. A few weeks during the summer they might use her. They don't care the way you and I do. I'm not blaming them. They have a right to the lives they want, but they'd never take time to pamper teak and brass. There's nothing sadder than a neglected boat."

She sat at the helm while he heated canned spaghetti over the alcohol burner. Even before her illness she disliked to cook. This last year he'd fixed most of the meals. He carried up her plate.

"Is it bad, what you're doing?" she asked.

"You think I'd do bad things to you?"

"Why then?"

"The purpose of cruising is not having to know why."

"Just as long as you won't drown me so you can run off with a blonde."

He laughed, but her face didn't change. It turned from him toward the port quarter and a sea tinged pink by sunset.

He started the engine to charge the batteries, and when she finished nibbling, he took her plate and cup below to wash them. Out of her sight he stood thinking, hesitant for the first time since they cast off. He considered going back. Then he fastened the plates and mugs in the wooden rack over the galley sink.

He felt tired from his watches but attempted to show no weariness to her. That night, as the vane piloted *Wyndor*, he dozed. When he lifted his head, he heard her in the cabin.

He backed down the companionway to find her at the radio, the mike in her hand. He pulled the jack and thumbed the toggle to OFF. She said nothing and crossed to her berth, where she lay with her eyes open.

In the morning the wind veered, and he felt the first cold. It was a chill from ice—startling and primordial. He helped Belle into her heavy socks, seaboots, a wolverine-lined parka. He drew gloves over her hands.

"Why bother?" she asked, sitting passively on her berth.

"Dumb question."

"If you're discarding me, what difference does it make?"

"We're just sailing."

"Till what?"

"Till we stop."

He climbed to the cockpit. Wearing a brown knit cap pulled low over her ears, she came up slowly. He offered his hand, but she wouldn't take it. She sat forward, a shoulder leaned against the cabin. Whitish sunlight glossed her skin. She surprised him by laughing.

"The first time we sailed together, you were showing off for me," she said. "You couldn't raise the anchor and were tugging on the rode. When it gave, you did a rear somersault into Boston harbor."

"At least I never mistook Vineyard Sound for Buzzard's Bay."

"The charts had blown overboard."

"You almost rammed the light tender."

For a few moments they were back to a time when they possessed strength and quickness, when glorious reflex preceded thought. They won a regatta, danced at the boat club, and in a green anchorage made fine tipsy love that produced their first child.

She raised her face to stare at a ship that would cross their bow, a large vessel, black with raked white stacks. He headed up so that *Wyndor* would pass well astern.

"You think I meant to swim for it?" she asked.

"Avoiding wake."

"What did the doctors tell you?"

"Let's not ruin this good air with doctor talk."

"They must've told you something. The pain's worse."

"Increase your dosage."

"Did they say I was going to die?"

"I'm shortening sail."

"Unfair to tell you and not me."

The sea wasn't rough, but he fastened his safety harness before he doused the jenny and ran up a working jib. Once he could've poured a martini standing on a plunging bow.

When he returned aft, she lay under a blanket on her berth. Her eyes were open, but she didn't acknowledge him. He asked whether she wanted coffee. She shook her head.

At dusk, as he sat by the wheel smoking and trying to stay awake, he heard the plane. Possibly part of her radio transmission had gotten through. The aircraft banked against a blood sun and slowly circled, its silver skin flickering. He switched off his running lights.

Belle came topside and shielded her eyes to look. He didn't realize she carried a flare till she tried to ignite it. He held her arms, and the flare dropped into the water.

The plane kept circling, yet ever more distantly. He released Belle but didn't again switch on *Wyndor's* running lights. She stood watching the plane. She sat and pressed thighs like sticks against her hands.

"I took care of you," she said.

"You did indeed."

"You're an alcoholic. Without me you'd be dead."

"I haven't had a drink in eighteen months."

"But you want it, and without me you'd be in the bottle."

She watched him. She had eyes bluish gray, like the winter sea. He trimmed the main.

"You'll bungle it," she said. "When have you ever done anything right?"

"You were right."

"It was my money that bought the boat. It's been my money that's bought everything we've had."

Her face became hateful—sharp, vicious, transformed to an alien. Then she smiled, and he again saw in her the ghost of a lovely young girl on a float of white gardenias.

"But you were a stylish drunk," she said. "You never slobbered or fell."

"Thanks for that."

"I want a normal death where the doctors try everything."

"There's nothing normal about trying everything."

"I want to fight."

"That's what we're doing."

"Explain why you won't let me go my way."

He couldn't tell her he'd be unable to endure seeing her among those gaunt, terrified bodies connected to tubes and plastic bags, people who smelled of urine and fear, all living horrors, some hairless, others with great bites taken out of them by surgeons. The sea was the clean way.

"I'll check the knot meter," he said.

They were making five knots, on a close reach now, a good point of sail for *Wyndor*. The ocean's roll gave her a slightly yawing motion, but she rode high and easily over the capped waves.

While Belle slept, he drowsed at the wheel. He didn't see the boat till it was off the port beam and closing. He believed it must be the police, but through his binoculars he identified it as a fishing trawler, its diesels pushing it hard against the gray swells, the stern at times seeming to sink beneath the following sea. The boat's dark outriggers had been secured to the mast.

The trawler approached within fifty yards and ran a parallel course. On the pilothouse bridge stood two men, one with raised binoculars. Chris waved, fearing they might hail him, wake Belle, and bring her on deck, where she could cry for help. The trawler, however, bore off westward, its horn giving a single short toot. Belle didn't come up from below.

Wind gusted and the waves shortened, changing *Wyndor*'s motion to jerkiness. He grew colder. Cold was what he wanted. He went below to see about Belle. She shivered on her berth. He lit the kerosene stove and zipped her into her sleeping bag.

He heated soup to feed her. Carrying a mug, he went topside to check the vane. Night was on them. As he adjusted course, the sea hissed and rose about him like a black wall. In dim moonlight he saw *Wyndor* was surrounded by whales, their luminous bulks heaving out of water that sluiced over their arching backs. Blowholes wheezed, and lazy flukes slapped the ocean.

He went for Belle, drew her from the bag, and brought her up to the cockpit so she could watch. For thirty minutes they sat holding each other while the whales escorted them, one close enough to rasp the hull. He and Belle smelled the sweetish odor of sea mammals' breath.

Just as quickly as they'd appeared, the whales left, dark lumps smoothing out under the sliding water. Still he and Belle sat till she needed medicine. He brought her the bottle of capsules and a cup of tea. She was shaking from cold. He helped her below and again zipped her into the bag. She drew up her knees.

Wind tested *Wyndor*'s stiffness. Chris eased the helm five degrees, no longer worried about a precise course as long as it was generally northward. The first flakes of snow slanted against his face. He needed heat. In the cabin he rubbed his hands over the stove and sat by Belle to reach into her sleeping bag. She was warm, but he'd disturbed her.

Wind punched *Wyndor* and shifted. He went topside to douse the jib and reef the main. When he removed his gloves, his shaky fingers became so cold they were like wooden stubs. For once he desired the furler reefing of modern glass boats. He recleated his sheet and adjusted the vane.

Again snow blew at him, grits felt more than seen. Wind was reaching gale force, and cold had become a hunter stalking him. Gulping hot coffee generated no warmth.

The disturbed sea swirled, a chaos of dark water and blown spray.

He no longer trusted the vane to keep them from broaching. He considered heaving to, yet stayed at the helm. The storm might be of long duration, and drift could send them back too many miles.

He lifted his face and welcomed the storm. If this did it, fine. In the sea they couldn't live more than a few minutes, and cold was, after all, the best way. Months ago he'd decided freezing was. He'd read up on the subject. Once a person made it through the doorway of initial pain, he came upon warmth, ease, and rest.

Belle kept to her berth during the night. He beat his arms against his wobbling body and stamped his seaboots. Time and again he went to the stove. Berries of ice grew on his beard and eyelashes. Sinuous black water rose and spat at the boat, the coiling and release of a great serpent.

The knockdown came at dawn, a combination of his falling asleep, a mighty gust, and a rogue wave. He'd fastened himself to the steering pedestal with his safety line, yet was thrown from the boat and sank choking. *Wyndor* righted herself and pulled him back into the cockpit.

Though the cockpit was draining, sea had spilled through the hatch and down the companionway. Staggering and as rigid as a man without joints, he started the engine and pump.

Belle had fallen from her berth. She lay in sloshing water. The stove fire had been quenched. When he struggled to lift her, he felt her limpness through the nylon fabric of the sleeping bag. He believed she must've hit her head and pushed her wet hair off her brow as he bent to her mouth. There was no breath. Her head rolled.

She had left him.

Capsules floated about. She could have swallowed an overdose, or maybe it was the cold or final flowering of the evil growth within. Not that it made a difference. He arranged her on the berth and tucked a blanket tightly around the bag to hold her. His numb fingertips drew down her eyelids.

He fought his way topside as wind slashed the reeling *Wyndor*. Colliding gray waves foamed against the revolving sky. Chunks of ice, like crystal hogs, wallowed in swells. Snow twisted against his face, and he wept into the biting flakes, letting his tears come fully at last.

The pump emptied the cabin, and he shut off it and the engine. He'd planned burial at sea. He would read the sailors' words over Belle and give her to the waves. He could then beat southward or issue a distress call. If he survived, there would be inquiries. He feared no charges against himself. Rather, he wanted to bring no publicity or disgrace to Belle's last days.

He stumbled to the wheel. The hunter's relentless fingers felt for the center of him. He held course, sailing *Wyndor* into a morning spitting pearls. More spray froze on his quaking face. He pried at his eyes to keep them open.

Sun flashed so dazzlingly the brightness was pain through his skull. Snow whipped him and the boat, and at moments the sun and snow twined.

He hurt. He whimpered. Oh God the cold! He lacked the courage to step through its doorway. He allowed *Wyndor* to run free and skid into swirling troughs. He sat facing the sparkling, iced rigging. The reefed mainsail flapped and popped into shreds with a sound like a gunshot. He didn't try to tend it. He hardly felt himself tip forward.

Light roused him, piercing light he'd never known before, a clean, cutting whiteness that sliced from all directions. He attempted to lift his head from deck snow and for an instant believed he must be passing through a gantlet of judgment in the court of the gods—majestic, white-robed divines, who loomed with resplendent grace on a tossing, steel blue sea.

I'm already dead, he thought, yet struggled to push to his knees. He wished to appear properly worshipful in the silver halls of this glittering kingdom of ice.

moon lady

She danced on the fragrant alluvial bank of Virginia's woods-bounded Weeping River, in a circular clearing where once young people had driven with their smokes, guitars, and six-packs to frolic in the rite of youth—where I myself had journeyed only a short time ago, or what seemed it, for I was now less than a month from forty.

I did not like to think of forty.

During the night I slipped from my parents' frame house, which gleamed like milk under the moon. My visit to them was a semiannual duty call, and in the clean, scuffed room of the second floor I'd been unable to sleep because of late-August air stinging my skin like nettles.

Outside the screened window, tree toads squatted among lichenous branches of oaks to voice the hot pulse of the night. On a limb of a thirsty, drooping mimosa a mockingbird commenced and broke off a flight of song, tripping over the intricacies of his too ambitious melodic line.

My loafers in hand, I moved softly through the drum-taut house, past my parents' bedroom, where I heard my father snore, and out through the kitchen, smelling of salt-rising bread and country meats. Then across the squeaky back porch and down steps to grass parched under my feet, the sound of its crackling seeming loud enough to wake not only my parents, but also people in the village—the few people in "the town of the dead," as we, the young ones, used to call it in our yearning to be away. I still thought of Dry Branch in that manner.

Loafers on, I walked the dusty shoulder of the moonlit pavement, which was also a secondary highway, past the colored cemetery where tombstones glowed. I allowed my feet to carry me southward down the cedar lane that led to the hidden river.

The lane had grown up, brambles, thistle, and hawthorn sneaking in to capture it back. No longer did gals and boys in search of joy keep the path cleared. The legs of my tan slacks would be weed-stained and speckled with beggar lice.

The moon laid a sheen on the burnished blackness of the river, the water appearing to rest rather than flow. It quietly rasped the banks. The woods smelled of honeysuckle and moist loam. Still present was the great peeling birch dangling a Manila rope on which we'd swung out over the river and dropped howling, wiggling as if we'd been tossed off a cliff and were falling to destruction. Only part of the rope, high up, remained.

As I stood under the birch's deeper darkness and looked past branches pleading to the moon, a shape stepped from the downstream woods, a woman slim and straight, not so much walking as gliding stiffly, as if she were part of a procession, her arms rigid at her sides, her legs unbending, her shoulders squared.

She stood in the clearing and gazed at the moon. My guess was she'd left her man among moss and ferns where he lay repairing his passion after a session of love.

I thought of a girl I'd brought here, her name Lois Anne, and how the act for both of us had been not so much one of affection or discovery as a desperate thrusting to break free from the barren, killing countryside, as if we through screwing could rocket out of ourselves into a worldly life of meaning and magic, of style and grace.

The woman still peered at the moon. Slowly, arms extended, she raised her palms. She began to sway to an unheard music. Arms lifted, she toed off sandals and drifted into a stately dance. Flat-footed she leaned left, then right, and spun long and languidly. The only sound was that of her feet passing through dust.

She was a slender, astonishing shape, her hair swinging lazily about her hips. Her skin caught the moon glaze, a silvery phosphorescence. She hummed, not a song but a beat, as if her voice were a tom-tom tapped gently with the fingertips. Her body was a sinuous flow.

No lover from the woods joined her. Maybe none lay in the honeysuckled darkness, no spent, rural Casanova refueling out of a cooled can of Budweiser. This was a ritual, a liturgy in which the woman was priestess, celebrant—a pagan service performed on the outskirts of Christian terrain, she a southern bacchante conjuring a demon lover on the very threshold of the upright Baptists.

Her arms slowly lowered, yet still she danced. She wore a simple, bright shift pinched at the waist by a belt. Solemnly she acted as if warding off hands, though the hands were her own. The belt loosened and dropped into the dust behind her.

The shift, now more like a robe, shimmered under the moon. Her dance became a luminous silhouette. She moved more quickly, frantically, and her elbows lifted. She pushed at hands, keeping them off until fingers found buttons and freed them. She backed away from herself, her palms protesting, her feet raising plumes of dust.

When the dress slid down her body, she closed her eyes and again raised her face to the moon. She wore no undergarments and appeared rigidly virginal. Tensed, defiant, she balled her hands into fists and turned her face aside.

The hands unclenched, moved along her hips, over her stomach, and cupped her breasts. Fingers circled her nipples. Her face came down, the body softened. She exhaled as if breath were endless.

I stood where coiled birch roots had long ago buckled the earth and somebody had shattered a bottle, dark shards of which clinked against soles of my loafers.

She whirled and stared. She crouched to snatch up her dress, belt, and sandals. She ran downstream among trees, her body a fleeting whiteness.

I stood hearing the whispering of the river and shrill of night insects. What had I seen? I turned in a circle, waited, and finally walked back along the lane, stepping into shaggy, motionless cedar shapes laid down by the moon. From time to time I stopped to listen.

•

In the morning I lay in the bed and wondered whether the woman had been a dream. I ran fingers over my loafers. They were filmed with dust of the river-bottom land. Their smell was alluvial. I sat on the rickety porch of my parents' house, where trellised rosebushes filtered the early sunlight. Who could she be? Again I pictured the sinuous dance under the moon.

Surely she wasn't from this village of the old, of the dead, where minutes crept like woolly worms laboring across the rounded, moss-mortared bricks of the front walk. Dry Branch had been a tobacco town, the county seat, where wagons had lined up for miles to deliver their fire-cured leaf to the auctions. Now the acrid, shadowy warehouses were in what our country folk called cities, places like Danville, South Boston, and Lynchburg, all of which had shopping centers, movies, and respectable women who wore pants.

Dry Branch was named after a sometime creek that ran through the village to the river. The best and boldest of the young left as soon as their legs were strong enough to carry them, as I had left, first to go to the Navy, then to college, and finally to my job as assistant editor of the *Virginia Travel Magazine*.

"I always hoped you'd be a professional man," my mother said, by which she meant a schoolteacher, for there was no possibility of my becoming a doctor or lawyer, neither the talent nor money being at hand. I never considered the ministry, my call being not to the church but to the roadhouses, the ladies, and the illusion of finding a golden land around the bend.

My mother was a small woman, yet not weak. Reared on a farm, she had milked, butchered, and suckered tobacco with the men. Though in her late fifties, her arms were still hard as planks, and she could lift heavy sacks of chicken scratch with the rhythmical ease of a field hand—a person who not only used his muscles efficiently but was also in communion with them.

For so long she dreamed I'd be a preacher. She'd love me to the

grave, yet she believed I lived a sinful, riotous life in Richmond—
first, because I'd been divorced; second, because of leggy Bess, a
perfumed buyer for a department store who once shared my apartment and had the bad luck while dressed in peach lounging pajamas to
open the door when my mother came calling unannounced.

My mother gaped, tightened her mouth, and walked off without a
word. She was in Richmond at the State Convocation of the Women
of the Church. She and my father were Presbyterians. Though Dry
Branch's population was less than five hundred souls, the village
supported seven churches, each with its own cemetery. In my mother's eyes I had fallen, and she was terrified I might be lost eternally.
Often she prayed over me.

"Or you ought to go into civil service," my father said, by which
he meant a government job. A farm-equipment mechanic, he smelled
of gasoline, exhaust fumes, and the crop in harvest. He'd passed
through hard times, and to him a dependable income and irrevocable
pension meant more than security—it meant being a member of an
earthly elect who achieved rapture here and now.

Maybe the dancer was some single live spirit attempting to rise
from the valley of dry bones, though Dry Branch had no valleys. The
land was supine, and the river moved as if uncertain in what direction
gravity pulled it. Perhaps the dancer sought to invoke the gods to
strike the countryside with beauty, promise, and fulfillment, to set a
sea in a desert.

We had in Dry Branch a red courthouse with white columns, a
stone clerk's office protected by an iron door, and a Confederate
monument around which the ladies planted daffodils. The treading
bronze soldier was beloved by breasty pigeons, birds as shiftless as
the idle men, black and white, who sat and gossiped in shade of
mistletoed elms growing decrepitly from the courthouse lawn.

I strolled around wondering about the moon lady. Each woman I
passed I eyed, though few were young. Women of any kind were
seldom seen walking. They drove in their husbands' or boyfriends'
pickups to the store, market, or county cannery, where they put up
snaps, butterbeans, and pickled okra.

I sat on the brick retaining wall around the courthouse lawn, which was cooled slightly by the thin shade dropped by the elms. I smoked and watched till lunchtime. I didn't see what could be called a pretty young woman, much less an untamed, wanton one who would shed her dress and offer her breasts to the moon.

Fled I had years before from Dry Branch, yet I still knew most everybody in the village. No change here. I knew them outside the village too, along the dusty, rutted roads and in the bled fields, where stalks of pulled tobacco stood like gaunt sentinels in a defeated land.

People spoke my name and I theirs. We conversed about rain, crops, and the price of cattle as if I'd never left. Years gone meant nothing. Since I'd been born in the county, I would always belong to it.

"Anybody new in town?" I asked my mother, who was fixing me an egg sandwich for lunch. She wore white socks and flowered bedroom slippers around the house. She kept a pair of shoes near the front door so if company or the preacher came to call she could get decent in a hurry.

"The Jacksons have another daughter, this one fine, a tiny little thing with a full head of black curly hair," she said. The Jacksons were a sawmill operator and his wife. "Sweet she is, smiles at everybody."

"I'm not talking about babies."

"What's newer than a baby?" she asked.

I dozed on the porch glider and in my mind journeyed up and down the roads, house by house, attempting to think of wives and daughters, all of them, their names and what they looked like. Who among them would have the craziness to perform the elaborate moonlit ritual? I wondered too what she would have done, what final orgiastic rite, had she not been spooked by me.

"Anybody new in town, I mean young and, you know, worth using your eyes on?" I asked Monk Randolph, a sheriff's deputy, who joined me for a smoke in the elm shade. Monk bordered on being albinic, his eyes pinkish, his head and body covered with a whitish fuzz. We'd gone to school together through the tenth grade, when

Monk quit to help his father on the farm. Monk's feet were heavy over this earth, as if they distrusted rising from it, but he too wanted to escape Dry Branch.

"Who'd come to this place except to shrivel up and die?" he asked. "I'm going to take the State Police exam. Maybe I can still get out."

"Nobody at all?"

"Bunch of hippies bought a tract on the Poorhouse Road, but they supposed to have hightailed it back to the rocks they crawled out from under of."

Hippies, sure, had to be, the girl maybe popping pills and flying and doing her mad dance beside the river. In my Ford I drove along the Poorhouse Road, sticky asphalt sprinkled with white gravel. Grasshoppers leaped from weeds and pinged against the car.

The Moses tract, Monk had said, and I remembered the farm where black, plodding Mrs. Moses had grown gigantic strawberries so luscious the stinging sweetness sped up through my teeth to my nose and skull, causing a cloying fireworks.

The barbed-wire fences were rusty and bowed, and the fields had soured and gone to broomstraw, it curving slightly in a southwest breeze. The house, a one-story box built around a chimney and set on stones, was sway-backed. Windows were shattered, and bricks missing from the flue.

The gray wood siding was pocked by woodpeckers drilling for borers. The front door had fallen in among broken glass. I found an upturned three-legged milking stool, a yellow comb, and a heelless shoe. There was also an outdated wall calendar picturing a tall, tanned brunette naked except for a motorcycle helmet and boots. The calendar advertised auto parts.

I drove away through the prickly pigweed. At the paved road a farmer stopped his pickup to look at me with the honest curiosity of a country man. It was Mr. Dan Wallace, ancient of days, whom I'd pitched hay for as a boy. He'd been frugal to the point of carrying even his pennies in a leather purse pocketed in the breast of his overalls, and had paid us only twenty cents an hour.

"Having wild parties and carousing," he said, lips stained purple-brown by snuff. "All time of night you could hear them and their motorcycles. Deer season some of the local hunters pulled up and cut loose with their shotguns. Them hippies left so fast they didn't even bend the grass."

"Girls too?" I asked, thinking it'd been lead pellets that pocked the gray warped siding of the house, not woodpeckers.

"Girls was the worst, lying naked in the fields to sun themselves, but they all gone now. Riffraff 'round here becoming worse than bull thistle."

He spat and worked his lower lip to adjust and squeeze juice from the snuff.

"Were they pretty?" I asked.

"Pretty? They was dirty, smelly, ugly, God almighty, they'd make a toad puke!"

He adjusted his sweat-darkened felt hat and drove on along the sunny road in his pickup, a Chevy, like him aged, creased, and palsied.

•

Returning to Dry Branch, I wondered whether one of the hippie girls hadn't left and might be hiding in the woods. Not likely. She'd have to eat. Somebody would've seen her going to the river or coon hounds have sniffed her out. And the moon lady had been pretty, my impression anyway.

I passed a clutter of shanties and junked cars strung down a red road. Peering into a rural mailbox was a stylish young negress wearing black highheels, tight white pants, and a shocking-pink tanktop. She gave me the death look of reverse discrimination.

I considered whether it might've been a black sister romping under the moon. In such a light, the silverish glaze, her ginger skin tone would not be distinguishable. Again I pushed my mind back to reconstruct the scene.

I shook my head. I couldn't accept it. Racist I wasn't, unlike my father, a classic stereotyper, but there were features, ways of moving, a certain lilting gait, and, most important, the high African buttocks—all missing.

In the village I stopped at the post office—a white frame building not much larger than a smokehouse. Over the doorway an American flag hung as stiffly as tin. Miss Mortisse Payne, the postmistress, stood behind the counter as if guarding entrance to the promised land.

She was an erect, brittle little woman who seemed to be forever consulting postal regulations, her mouth set thin and bloodless. Auburn hair speckled with gray was pulled so tight it reined her face to smoothness, like cotton fabric drawn to tautness.

She'd known what in Dry Branch passed for tragedy, had been engaged to Mason Tucker, who was supposed to be the wildest boy who ever came from the county. He drank, got knifed gambling, backed up a truck and released cattle into corridors of the consolidated high school, sold the cheerleaders on a game of strip poker at the rear of the school bus, and spent thirty days in jail for fastening a brassiere around the breasts of the forever-treading Confederate statue.

What saved him from prison or an angry father's shotgun blast was the war. Mason was born to be a hero. He flew his crippled B-24 Liberator bomber not back toward the landing field but into the bridge of a Japanese light cruiser, head-on and still talking. His last words over the radio were "Tell that pretty little redhead gal I love her."

That pretty little redhead gal was Miss Mortisse Payne. Shortly thereafter she was left alone in this world by the death of her father. Through the benign machinations of Senator Harry Flood Byrd the elder, she was appointed Dry Branch's postmistress. The job was her balm in Gilead.

"I'm not authorized to give that information," she said when I asked about people recently arrived in the county. "And you might consider saving your government money by mailing out the change-of-address forms given you on more than one occasion."

She was peeved she had to readdress an infrequent letter from a Navy buddy or a subscription appeal from a forgotten magazine. Her handwriting was surgical; she used a government-issue pen, the spite evident in the ink and etched stroke, as if she were engraving steel instead of marking envelopes.

"I'll try to straighten up, Miss Mortisse."

"I have all I can do."

Driving out to John's Place, I passed Howell County High School, braked, and pulled my Ford into shade of a white-limbed sycamore tree. On matted grass in front of the main building the majorettes were practicing.

They were wearing not their golden boots and spangled briefs but shorts, T-shirts, and multicolored hairbands. They strutted bare-footed, and their batons spun sparkling up into sunlight, causing a flight of crows to caw and veer across the yellow sky.

I studied the prancing girls. Each was as dewy as a peeled peach, yet none possessed the sinewy grace of the luminous silhouette by the river. That person had been fully ripened in the ways of women, while these high-stepping, giggling girls were merely playing at the game of bodies.

I received a disapproving stare from their hip-heavy female coach, who wore a baseball cap, sweat pants, and a whistle. I drove on to John's Place, a chartreuse cinder-block roadhouse whose doorway was flanked by soft-drink machines.

Inside, deer heads decorated the walls, the animals' button eyes dimmed by dust. On a shelf behind the counter a plastic clock shaped like a black cat grinned, the cat's tail a pendulum that swung a red tongue from side to side of the mouth.

At John's Place you could buy a skinny hamburger, canned chili, and fresh chitlins during hog killing, but the reason for the roadhouse was beer. My parents would never allow me to drink at home, not even a little wine for the stomach, though they knew I drove out to John's.

"One beer for one queer," John said, his standard opening to all customers. He moved in front of me as I sat on a stool at the counter. He'd once played first base for the Danville Gobblers but, released, came back to Dry Branch, where the county reclaimed him and wore him down to its own.

He wore khaki pants and a long-sleeve white shirt, the collar open, the sleeves rolled up. He was no longer fleet now but fat, droopy of flesh. Movement was laborious and caused sweat to seep from pores and bead on sandy hair follicles along his arms and on the backs of his soft, pawlike hands.

While I drank beer from the bottle, John came around the counter to sit beside me. Taped to a mirror were baseball photos of him, one with his arm around Dizzy Dean. Nobody else was in the place because at two on a weekday afternoon in Howell County, not even ne'er-do-wells caroused openly. They had their code, which explained furtive draws from pint bottles in the shadows of secret places.

I asked John about new people, and he too mentioned the hippies. He then remembered a schoolteacher who'd just signed up for the fall term, a young girl who lived not in Howell but in King Charles, the adjoining county to the northwest.

"Saw her leaving the superintendent's office," John said. "Sweet itty-bitty thing. The rest of them's dog, pure dog."

"Name?"

"Culley. Mary Lou Culley. Her father owns the mill. Buy my rock salt and calf feed there."

I drove to Tobaccoton, county seat of King Charles, where tin roofs of abandoned, grimy warehouses smoldered under the sun and pigeons sought the deep shade of eaves. A phone book at the Dodge and Plymouth dealer's listed Mr. Culley's home address on Ridge Street. Ridge of what? I wondered. Tobaccoton didn't have even a hill.

The house was a new brick colonial with small English boxwoods planted along the walk and a concrete birdbath in the yard. The front door was open, some of the windows too, and from inside came music with a hard beat. I also heard the sound of a vacuum cleaner.

The moon lady didn't, I realized, have to live here, the sweet itty-bitty thing. She could have her own residence. I stepped to the screen door and knocked on its aluminum frame.

From dusk of the hallway came the girl, a blonde wearing tennis shoes, blue shorts, and a lavender blouse, the tail tied in a knot at her tanned young stomach. No, I thought. She was pretty enough but too tiny. The length of her hair would never swish around her hips.

"Mr. Culley in?" I asked.

"He stays at the mill till five," she said. Her small hand was lifted to the latch on the storm door, and with a painted thumbnail she teased an engagement ring. Her shoulders swayed slightly to the music.

I thanked her, drove back to Dry Branch, and began to believe I'd never left my parents' house that night, that the moon lady had indeed been a dream or vision.

•

My mother came from her garden at the back of the house, carrying a bucket of butterbeans. We sat at the kitchen table, and I helped shell them, the hulls cracking like knuckles.

Later I hoed the garden. That pleased her. I picked a tomato from the heavy vine and bit into its juicy flesh while it still held the sunshine's warmth. Sweating, I walked around to the shade of the front porch, reared my feet to the white railing, and sipped a glass of mint iced tea.

A car passed, engine popping, a creamy Porsche convertible, the driver a woman whose glossy black hair strung behind her in the wind. I thrashed forward to set my glass on the railing, hurried to my Ford, and took out after her.

By the time I got in gear, she was already well down the highway, traveling south fast. Only because she had to slow behind a tractor pulling a gleaner could I draw close. When she curved around the gleaner, I gave chase.

She's merely driving through Dry Branch, I thought, on her way to Danville or South Boston. I was just able to keep her in sight. At her speed we were at the county line in minutes. No use going farther, I thought, but even as I gave up and relaxed my foot on the accelerator, her brake lights flashed, and she turned onto a newly graded road between pod-hung locust trees.

The road led to a rail fence and stone gateposts providing entrance to a winding drive along which dogwoods had been planted. For an instant I didn't recognize the old Whorley place, where I'd hunted as a boy—rabbits, quail, and turkeys that burst from the lespedeza like bombs. The house had been gutted and windowless then, but now its yellowness dazzled. The roof was pale blue, and the four chimneys had been acid cleaned and pointed up.

I passed piles of sand and gravel as well as construction equipment. Shrubbery had been pruned and grass sown. The hole in the ground would be a swimming pool, and down from the ivy terrace was a tennis court surrounded by a gleaming cyclone fence into which wisteria had already twined.

She'd driven behind the house, where the board-and-batten stables had been restored and painted, also yellow. I stopped my car, backed, and drove to the highway and County Line Mercantile, a ramshackle one-room store covered by red imitation brick siding. Under the sagging overhang stood a single low-test gas pump.

Inside, a bald black man with a trimmed white moustache and a green butterfly bowtie was lifting eggs from a galvanized bucket and fitting them into paper cartons. The wooden counter was worn as smooth as bone. The place smelled of hams curing.

"She and her man been fixing it," he said.

"Who?"

"They bought down here from up north. He owns a plane he flies right over trees into a field. First time I saw it I thought he crashed."

"What's his name?"

"They not been around here long enough yet to have names."

I returned to the Whorley place, parked on the circular drive, and tucked in my shirt before crossing to the door—double doors, each with a brass knocker shaped like a swan. On either side of the entranceway were carriage lamps lacking bulbs.

The woman opened the door. She had on straw espadrilles, hip-hugging jeans, and a slate-colored workshirt with ivory buttons down the front and at the cuffs. Her left hand held a framed painting of a galloping chestnut horse.

"Excuse me for bothering you," I said, "but I'm lost in the wilderness and wondered how in the world a man finds the road to Danville."

She listened without moving. Her eyes were even blacker than her hair, and her skin had an inner darkness—Greek or Italian, I thought, or maybe Spanish. She wore pearl earrings set in gold.

"You've been following me," she said.

"I won't try to lie out of it," I said, and gave her my best smile. "Here in the county we don't have a lot to do except mind other people's business."

"I have a gun," she said, and brought the other hand from behind her. She cocked the hammer of a nickel-plated .32 caliber revolver. "I completed a course in how to use it and shot the knee off a man who tried to burgle our house."

"Hold your fire, lady, I'm leaving," I said, backing away, my hands up to show their emptiness. I sidled to my car, drove around the circle, and sped out. She was still looking after me and holding the gun.

Just as I reached the highway, Monk Randolph swerved his brown-and-tan police cruiser in front of my Ford. The siren shrilled, and red lights blinked and flashed. His car fishtailing, he kicked open his door and drew his pistol as he ran toward me.

"You didn't tell me about her," I explained.

"I never seen or talked to her except a while ago on the phone," Monk said, breathing hard and pushing his cap up with the pistol barrel. "She's practically out of the county anyhow, and just what the hell you think you're doing?"

"Checking my night vision," I said.

•

At my parents' house, in my room and with my shoes off, I considered the dark lady holding the gun. I now knew her name was Busalis and that she and her husband were from Cleveland, Ohio. They had bought the Whorley place to raise Arabian horses. Mares were to be vanned down when pastures were planted and fencing completed.

I concluded she was not the sinuous dancer in the moonlight. There was no sense to it. To reach the clearing she would've had to travel twenty-five miles back to the village. Why would she come all the way here in the middle of the night when she could've walked down the slope in front of her house to the river and do all the dancing she wanted? Moreover, she was too tough. She had the shape all right and might bump and grind. But conjure the moon? Never.

So where was I? Nowhere.

Before driving back to Richmond on Sunday, I was expected to attend church with my parents. During the night, rain blew in, tapping the tin roof, and the morning dawned dismally, though the air was still warm. It smelled of wetted dust. Pale golden leaves from the black-walnut tree fluttered to the grass. The walnut was always last to put out its leaves and first to lose them.

Our church building was 120 years old, its sun-kilned bricks weathered and pitted. Two aisles led under balconies where slaves had sat. The windows, pews, and pulpit were bare in the Presbyterian fashion, the minister, like everything else in the village, elderly—a Mr. Thurston Jamerson, who believed more in justice than in mercy. "God cannot tolerate sin anymore than water can tolerate fire" was his favorite theme.

Who the hell knew? Maybe he was right.

I half listened to his intricate, rebuking discourse and looked out a window to the wet tombstones of the graveyard. I again felt the pain of Bess's leaving me, not for another man but because, she said, "You are becoming spiritless and drawing in the walls." I thought of returning to those walls, an extinguished one-bedroom apartment, lifeless, with newspapers, TV schedules, and beer cans about. Two women I had lost, and I'd thought of myself as a great lover.

I was almost forty.

The congregation rose to sing. As we lifted our faces to "O God, Our Help in Ages Past," the wet gloominess of morning was pierced by a sweep of sunlight. The light came so fast it was a flood of radiant brilliance, and I felt the quick warmth on my skin.

When I turned from the blazing window, my eyes full of swirling sun specks, I saw the woman who'd danced by the river. She sat near the front on the right-hand side of the nave. In the expanding brightness her shape was flat as a blade. She stood with fingers resting on the back of a pew, a knee bent inward, it pulling the rest of her slim body into a lovely curve. Glorious light streamed about her.

I squinted to clear my eyes. How had I missed her? I'd already counted the house and seen the familiar people. She hadn't walked in late or entered from the choir door. She seemed to have materialized by the window.

Then clouds massed, and the sunlight shut off as swiftly as it had scythed us. For a few seconds my eyes were still fired. The woman settled into focus. The hymn ended, and she sat with prim dignity, dabbing at her hair.

I sucked in my breath, and my parents glanced at me. It couldn't be, not Miss Mortisse Payne, our brittle little postmistress robbed of love by a hero's death, her spine a sword, her skin like fine linen long laid in a closed chest, her hair not a flinging bacchante's but a tight reddish gray bun. Unloosed, would that hair drop around her like a veil?

I was unable to stop watching, and after the service, while the congregation mingled under the oaks, I circled her as one might a creature dropped from the sky. Her dress was brown and plain, her shoes black and low heeled, her hat a dark straw platter. She lived close to the church and walked back toward her house as if hearing a marching beat. She clamped her pocketbook under an arm. Golden leaves of a walnut tree slanted about her.

"What's wrong with you?" my mother asked, resetting her glasses to peer at me.

"I've seen the light," I said.

" 'Bout time," my father said.

When we'd eaten our Sunday chicken dinner, I sat with my parents an hour on the porch before saying good-by. I kissed my mother, shook my father's roughened hand, and swung my suitcase up to the car's trunk. Leaving Dry Branch for Richmond, I slowed in front of Miss Mortisse Payne's house, stopped, and backed to it.

It was cleanly bleak, everything in place, like the post office. The windows seemed to stare with prudish, disapproving eyes, yet on the porch were painted cans of flowers, and a canary cage hung from a hook screwed into a small square column. The Sunday Lynchburg paper lay folded on the green swing, where once she and the future hero might have embraced, if nothing more.

Miss Mortisse, wearing an apron, came from shadows of the house to answer my knock. She'd been baking, for a pall of flour covered her slim, proficient hands. Inner flesh of her chalky arms was eroded to the veins, but her lavender eyes were like wild Confederate violets that grew along the churchyard wall.

"I'll change those addresses so you won't be bothered," I said.

"You came to tell me that?" she asked, and gazed at me through the screen door.

She was so upright and controlled, yet I pictured her alone and loveless in this whited sepulcher, and I did an astonishing thing—a crazy, instinctive act of penance in expiation of the disdain youth holds for age. I pulled open the door, grasped a powdered hand, and kissed the palm. It tasted of flour.

"I'm sorry," I said.

"You lost your senses?" she protested, and jerked her hand free. She was confused, sputtering, and building to outrage.

Hot with embarrassment, I retreated from her porch toward my car. The taste of flour galled my mouth. I stumbled over the mounting block at the curb.

"Carousing on Sunday!" she called after me in disgust.

I fled to Richmond. And yet, and yet, for many a day in my lonely apartment I wondered whether under her anger and righteous grimace there remained fragments of a loving young girl, memories of slender shapes seen as if through a silvery misted distance. Did moonbeams still call forth the yearnings of a thwarted and forlorn maiden?

Welcome to the club, I thought, and late on a cold, moonlit December night I filled out the change-of-address forms she'd given me on more than one occasion.

cuttings

When Asbury bought the four acres of wooded land fronting a tidal creek, there was only the one oak, and that already dying. It'd never been a giant, possessing nothing like the soaring grandeur of the trees on Capitol Square in Richmond, which he passed daily on his drive to the office.

No, his oak struggled to endure among the yellow pines, hollies, and wind-twisted cedars that shaded the marginal land, land which several times a season was washed with salt water—whenever a nor'easter blustered into a high tide or a mighty storm heaved in the Atlantic.

The spring the land was cleared to build the cottage, he and his wife Janie spared the oak. They in fact positioned the cottage so that the tree's farthermost boughs laid shadows on decking to which burgundy leaves spiraled every fall.

Each season he, Janie, and the children watched the oak decline. It bravely put out buds, but fewer of them uncurled into dwarf leaves, and then the top of the tree died, its decay drawing a redheaded woodpecker to the feast, the bird in time sculpturing the highest part of the trunk into a rough, pocked resemblance of an eagle's head.

In their fourteenth year of owning the cottage, the oak did not meet the spring. Still Asbury wouldn't have it cut. The children's swing hung from its lowest limb, and Janie had strung up painted feeders that transformed the tree into a blazing boardinghouse for birds. Sunflower seeds spilled about like glossy rain.

They'd named the cottage Heron because the great primordial birds strolled the creek shallows on stilted legs. Gulls hovered, and terns splashed the water. Yearly, ospreys built nests in spaces between the red, triangular daymarkers of a channel that led to the Chesapeake Bay.

Like the herons, the cedar cottage was stilted, on pilings, with a stone fireplace, cypress wainscoting, and wicker furniture. Driftwood pieces the color of pearl were stuck about. Sometimes the place, airy with decking and glass, gave Asbury the sensation of winged flight among weltering boughs.

During early November a mean wind hissed in from the sea and broke many trees. The highest limbs were sheared from the oak. Asbury worried that its core was insect ridden and another storm might tip it to the cottage, where it would smash the roof.

He talked to Janie, a tall, limber blonde who coddled her slimness by jogging with him each morning around the cindered high-school track near their Richmond home.

"The birds will starve they've been on welfare so long," she said as she hemmed a white evening gown that shimmered across her knees. The dress belonged to their nineteen-year-old daughter, Jill, who was coming out that winter.

"We can hang feeders from other trees."

"It won't be the same."

Asbury intended to hire Hinton Beard to cut the oak. Hinton was a man from Virginia's hill country who'd come to Richmond to work at Philip Morris' hogshead mill. Weekends Hinton trimmed trees and did other jobs requiring chain saws and ladders. He was fair-skinned, with hands so large that even empty they seemed to be gripping bricks.

"Promised my ladies I wouldn't do no more climbing," Hinton said, a natural gentleman who hated to say no, as he was doing now to Asbury. "They claim I'm too old to be dancing around up there."

Asbury hadn't thought of Hinton as aging but rather as being weathered by time, like good wood. And if Hinton was old, Asbury himself had put on some years.

"I could do it," he said, making the remark without thought at the dinner table. Janie, Jill, and Rick picked it up, the boy in his second year at Hampden-Sydney, where he was on the tennis team. Both Asbury's children were tanned and bleached from lives beside the water. Aburst with the gold of youth, they had an easy, clean-limbed beauty that put them above the fray.

"Call the rescue squad!" Rick said.

"And the hospital!" Jill said.

"Don't forget the funny farm," Janie said.

"The idea seems to be I'm not capable of doing the job," Asbury said.

"The idea is you'd be idiotic to try," Janie said.

His annoyance carried over to the next day at Old Dominion Securities, the brokerage shop where he was a vice-president. He was forty-six, neither ancient nor physically inept. He jogged, swam, and sailed their 27-foot sloop *Sea Bird* with as much verve as anybody along the coast. His American-twist serve could still overpower all but the best club players.

On his way home Thursday he stopped at a hardware store and bought a Poulan chain saw with a 16-inch blade. The saw came in a black plastic case complete with a tool for adjusting the chain's tension and a book of instructions. He also purchased a red 2-gallon can for mixing fuel. He smiled, knowing that in the rural South the first chain saw was a rite of manhood.

He left the purchases in his Oldsmobile's trunk and mentioned nothing to the family. He said he wanted to drive down to the cottage on Friday to winterize the boat. Janie would be busy with Jill's debutante preparations, and Rick had a date for a party weekend at Hampden-Sydney.

"Stay off the bay," Janie said. "I don't like you being by yourself."

He drove from Richmond on a cold, sunny afternoon. The interstate led to Williamsburg and beyond, where he crossed the York River to good tidal odors. He opened a window to breathe air that for so many years he'd associated with the freedom of time off and vacations.

When he reached the cottage, built on a point at the end of a sandy road that crackled with crushed oyster shells, he parked underneath and carried his suitcase to the bedroom. A sliding glass door gave out onto a deck and a view to the harbor, the sandspit, and the bay, which in the fading light was a blue blackness severed by fleeting whitecaps.

He glanced at the oak, not yet ready to bring his mind to the job he'd attempt early in the morning, when the wind was down and he could work safely on a ladder.

He mixed a drink, and took it and his binoculars to the water's edge, where he swept the horizon for birds. Two dashing flights of canvasbacks speared across a silvered sky and curved into the bronze marsh. He returned to the cottage to light a fire, then tossed a salad and broiled a steak. Before going to bed, he walked the deck. The cottage was being punched by wind, which the oak limbs shredded to a keen.

At first light he was up. The wind had dropped and shifted from sea to land. Because the day was cold, he wore his leather boots, down vest, and knit cap. He walked around the oak, studying it. If the lean were right, he could saw it at the lower trunk, but the tree was definitely inclined toward the cottage.

He decided to trim the oak's top, whittle it down three or four feet at a time. He set his aluminum extension ladder against the trunk. From the car he lifted his saw. He reread the starting instructions and knelt to pull the cord.

The engine fired immediately and loudly, causing squawks from gulls who flapped away toward open water. He tried the blade on a piece of driftwood, and the saw passed through with ease, not seeming to cut as much as sink.

He switched off the engine, lifted a coil of nylon anchor line from a nail driven into a piling, and tied a bowline around the saw's handle. He placed the saw at the foot of the ladder and held the line as he climbed. When he reached the bottom limb, he stepped onto it and released the children's swing. He allowed it to fall. He unfastened the bird feeders and pitched them underhanded down into bayberry bushes.

He drew up the saw, tied the anchor line around the trunk, and began his ascent. The oak was no more than thirty feet high, yet before he was halfway to the top he realized he was moving clumsily and breathing hard. He also gripped limbs tightly.

He rested a moment and looked toward the bay. The tide was slack ebb, and seabirds rested along the glistening shore. A great blue heron perched atop the wooden frame of a crab trap at the marsh's edge, hoping for breakfast and raptly seized in a gaze of judgment.

He resumed his climb and again felt tired. The saw, which he'd been changing from hand to hand, was loose in his fingers. Was he sick? He wanted to go no farther. As he hesitated, a tremor passed through his body.

Why, he thought, you're afraid! He couldn't believe it. Heights had never troubled him. He'd been a fighter pilot who made a strafing run so low over a rice paddy that his air intake sucked up grain. His office was hung with an outsized picture of him and his squadron standing before a plane the nose of which had been painted to resemble an attacking shark.

The idea of fear made him angry, and he again started climbing, this time going up to the top third of the tree, high enough to think of trimming. He pulled on cotton gloves, wiped a sleeve of his flannel shirt across his mouth, and jerked the cord. The saw didn't fire, though he kept yanking at it. He was sweating.

Arms around the tree, he examined the saw. He'd forgotten the toggle switch. He thumbed it to the ON position. When he pulled the cord, the engine caught explosively and shot an oily blue vapor about him.

He slid a foot along a limb, brought weight to it, and the limb broke. He clutched the tree. He watched the limb fall and thought of himself dropping the saw and tumbling after it. He might land across the blade. No neighbor was near, and he could lie unconscious and bleeding.

God, he was actually shaking and felt weak to limpness. He switched off the saw. On the ground it hadn't seemed heavy, but up here it was stubbornly cumbersome and wanted to drag him down.

Disgusted with himself, furious, he started it again. He sliced off small limbs just to prove he could and swung the blade toward a large branch, but instead of parting cleanly, the branch fell in against his leg and knocked his foot loose.

He dropped the saw to hug the tree. The saw bounced and banged its way down till it snapped upward at the end of the anchor line, yet continued to run and buck. The blade flailed, finally scything the line. Even lying on its side, the saw functioned perfectly.

As he climbed down, he trembled, and the tree seemed made of glass. Fear didn't stop at the ladder, which, like a child, he one-footed step by step. He righted the saw, switched it off, and wiped sweat from himself.

He sank to the ground and waited for his breathing to quiet. Unbelievable how his hands wobbled when he held them out. Over the hill at forty-six he was. Okay, he'd pack, lock the cottage, and return to Richmond. Go back to his desk and never tell his family or anyone.

No, damnit, he wasn't through with the tree. A few years ago he would've frolicked up the ladder and topped the oak without thought, knowing in the sureness of his muscles and the swift, instinctive moves of his body what was right. The saw would've been an extension of his arm and youth.

As he stood, he wondered what if he succeeded in climbing the ladder and topping the oak and the tree fell on him, swung in as the branch had done. Again he pictured himself lying comatose among bayberries, unmissed and unaided for days. He cursed. That's how age and maturity corrupted a man, made him think what if, what if.

Defeat or not, he wasn't climbing the ladder right now. Janie, Rick, or Jill might spot the work he'd already done and wonder. He could lie out of it, but the idea of being false to his family was shameful to him.

No, the tree had to come down. All right, he'd get help. He walked to his car, drove out along the sandy road past cottages empty for the winter, and stopped at the wharf near the head of the creek where watermen docked their boats. He'd offer money for a man to go up the tree.

No one was at the wharf, just the gulls with their rusty cries and the long, white dead-rise crafts locally built, battered outboards cocked to protect the propellers from mud at low tide. Some boats had wire crab pots stacked in them, others oyster tongs and nets. All needed bailing.

He drove to Bittern Marsh, the post office, a red board-and-batten building smaller than the den of his Richmond home. No stores or houses were nearby, just gray, loblolly-fringed fields stubbled with stripped soybean vines.

From the post office came a tall, muscled black wearing a felt hat, a blue pea jacket, and high rubber boots, his overalls stuffed into them. He was a waterman, a person who found his dollars on the creeks and bay, harvesting oysters, crabs, and fish—a farmer of the waters. Asbury smelled the sea on him before they were close enough to speak.

"Want me to do what?" the black man asked, his speech slurred through his nose after the fashion of peninsula people. "Climb your tree?"

Behind him at the door was the postmistress, a stout, graying woman named Horseley. She'd heard what Asbury wanted and would tell it as surely as if he'd paid to have it broadcast by radio. She would say the "come-here"—what the locals called outlanders—needed somebody to go up that little old tree because he was afeard to do it himself.

Or the black himself might give the story about among the community of watermen, and they would spit and nod with the knowledge that though they had not city money, fancy clothes, or foreign cars, they were made of enduring stuff which would keep them on the land or sea long after the litter of come-heres had blown away.

"Changed my mind," Asbury said, went to his car, and drove back to the cottage, where he looked at the oak. Though once fond of it, he hated it now. The tree had become an instrument of revelation—the closed door to his youth.

The hell with it, he'd go home. If Janie and his family found out about his attempt and failure, he'd confess, accept their greasy smiles, and trod to the refuge of his office. Men everywhere gave up to age and caution. No logic justified his being different.

He packed and drove all the way to Gloucester Point before slowing his Olds, curving away from the York River Bridge, and turning. He couldn't just quit and live with his cowardice. He went back to the cottage, twenty-three miles, stepped from the car, and smoked a cigarette as he stared at the tree.

There had to be another means of bringing it down, some system that would not require climbing at all. Wishful thinking. The oak was absolutely slanted toward the cottage.

For an instant he considered gambling. If he notched the tree on its far side, some combination of forces his eyes hadn't revealed might fell the oak obliquely so that it would miss the cottage a few inches.

No, it'd hit and do terrible damage. His impulse had risen from panic and desperation.

He circled the tree as one might a serpent. Suppose there was a device that would keep the oak from falling against the cottage even if the tree were cut at the trunk. Among pilings he'd stacked salt-treated lumber intended for use in building a new dock. He had nails, a hammer, a saw. In Richmond he was reputed to have brains.

From his lumber he slid a 2″ × 10″. He carried it to the second-story deck, propped one end at the base of a railing post, and jammed the other against the tree. So far, so good. Trouble was the weight of the oak might cause it to slip or roll around the brace.

He again went under the cottage, where he lifted a 2″ × 4″, which he sawed in half-lengths of fifteen inches each. He nailed the pieces to the 2″ × 10″ at an angle that forked them out over its corners, forming a Y with a long stem.

Okay, so what if he put the brace in the ready position and sawed the tree at ground level? The oak would still be leaned to the house. He needed a way of pulling the tree to make it miss the cottage.

Perhaps he could borrow a block and tackle from the watermen, though even then he'd have to climb the tree and attach the rope high. He didn't want to go up that ladder again into fear.

If he could push the tree, it was heavy, sure, but with a long timber forced against the top he'd have leverage, especially at the moment the tree was about to fall, the instant it was just in balance.

He went to his lumber pile for a twelve-foot 4" × 4", which he lugged to the upper deck and shoved out against the top of the oak— the eagle's head the woodpecker had carved. Part of the head crumbled and dropped, but an eye socket remained, seeming to express the tree's malevolent feeling for him.

He lifted the chain saw and walked to the oak. If it fell where he wished, it would topple into bayberry growth. He started the saw, yet hesitated. Returning home and hiring a professional to do the job would be so sensible. That's what professionals were for, and he was being stupid and mulish not to use them.

Well, stupidity and mulishness were sometimes required to salvage self-respect. He squeezed the pistol-like trigger and touched the shrilling blade to coarse ridges of the oak's trunk. He made his first cut horizontal and held the saw to its work till he was approximately halfway through the tree.

He pulled out the blade, released the trigger, and stepped back to look. If rotted at the center, the oak might collapse, but it stood solid against the sky's cold paleness, its dead branches not yielding to the rising wind.

He pushed at the tree with both hands. There was no sway even when he laid his shoulder against the trunk.

He now had to make his second cut, this one down at a 45° angle to the first. That's how the instruction booklet said to do it. The result would be a wedge taken from the tree in the direction he wanted it to fall.

When he began, the blade moved smoothly, but then stalled so that he had to horse it to keep cutting. He guessed the tree had settled slightly, pinching the bar, or the saw's teeth could've met a knot, some tangled grain of wood. He kept at it till the wedge popped out to the ground.

He pushed at the tree but felt no give. He inspected the gap the wedge had left. The cavity glistened cleanly. No sign of borers or rottenness.

It was time for the third and most important cut. The idea was to circle to the opposite side of the tree and saw on a plane that intercepted the gap, though higher than the first horizontal bite, creating a hinge that would allow him to tip the oak over.

He smoked and rested. He wanted to be calm when he did this. He thought how a surgeon must feel at the moment before he drew a scalpel across flesh. There could be no walking away once it was opened.

He wiped his hands, pulled his gloves tight, and readied the saw. The blade quivered as it touched the trunk. Part of him wanted to hurry while the rest drew back. He cut only a few inches before stopping and going up to the deck, where he raised the 4″ × 4″ and rammed it against the tree's top. The oak was not disturbed.

He went down, cut another two inches, and climbed to the deck. He pushed the 4″ × 4″ hard against the tree. Nothing. He was being too cautious with his saw—more than cautious, craven.

A third time he returned to the tree. As he started to cut, his saw stopped abruptly. He jerked the cord. The engine wouldn't catch. He unscrewed the black cap and found he was out of fuel.

He smoked and allowed the saw to cool before pouring gasoline from the red can. He filled the oil reservoir, which lubricated the groove of the cutting bar. The saw started at the first pull, no choke, and he stepped to the tree, where he fitted the blade into the cut. This time he went a good three inches deeper through the trunk.

He lowered the saw and climbed to the deck to push the 4″ × 4″ against the tree. Still nothing. He was wearing himself out on stairs.

As he again used the saw, he glanced at the top of the tree and shouted, believing the oak was falling on him. He jumped back and shoved the saw away. From the driveway he watched the tree. It wasn't moving. Rather, a mare's tail of cloud floating over had created the illusion.

His skin tingled, and he coughed. Because he felt he would give out if he didn't finish quickly, he lifted the saw, fitted it, and cut recklessly for twenty seconds. When he straightened, the only thing holding the oak was a hinge of trunk an inch-and-a-half thick.

Surely the oak would fall, yet when he ran up to the deck and pushed the 4″ × 4″, the tree resisted. He flung off his down vest and hurried to the ground for the saw. Just a kiss of the blade should be enough.

Delicately he worked the blade into the cut. He was tense and shaky. He used only a short burst of power, yanked out the saw, and rushed up to the deck.

He could've taken his time. The tree withstood the 4″ × 4″, though wind was assaulting it now, a result of the sun's heating the earth and causing an updraft to pull air from the sea.

He set his feet, breathed deeply, and bulled the 4″ × 4″. Was there a slight give? Upper limbs did quiver. No matter, the oak wouldn't go over. Yet if he left even for a second, wind might nudge it toward the cottage.

In a rage he cursed and pounded his body against the 4″ × 4″ one last time. The tree tilted. It didn't fall but was definitely tipped away from the cottage. The brace dropped to the ground.

He ran down the steps, started his saw, and sank the blade into the widened cut. The oak creaked, settled with ascending speed, and thudded among bayberry, its length lying exactly where he wished.

He was exultant. He laughed, whirled, and raised a triumphant fist. He went to the refrigerator for a beer and stood over the oak as if it were a fallen foe.

"By God, you did it!" he shouted. "You outsmarted it!"

He used the rest of the day for trimming limbs from the oak and sawing the trunk into sections of fireplace size. One winter morning he would bring a sledge and two iron wedges to split the sections for his woodpile.

That night, after two drinks and a dinner of frozen pizza, he stood on the deck. Wind blew from the northeast, carrying coldness and snow that flickered against running lights of a ship passing along the coast. He heard the somber buoy bell, but the keening of the oak was gone, as was its shape, leaving an emptiness in darkness.

He looked down to where the tree lay among the crushed fragrance of bayberry. For him nothing would ever again be as glorious as the daring move, the beautiful, thoughtless act, the sureness of muscle and reflex that preceded thought, the eye that knew before it measured.

Yet he'd been compensated for the loss, paid for the seized swiftness and certainty with a mind able to cope. If what he'd achieved was not quite victory, neither was it a rout.

In the morning he woke to find snow on the land and marsh right to the water's edge, where the tide had washed it. He locked the cottage, put his things in the car, and drove away.

He slowed to glance back through steam from his exhaust. The exhilaration was gone now. He remembered the oak in summer leaf above the cottage's shingled roof. A gentle, aching sadness entwined with a descending peace. Like the tree, time was sawing at him; and like the oak, too, he would endure until fallen, he hoped with a portion of its dignity, will, and strength.

smoke

I stood waiting on the broad front porch of the two-story white-frame farmhouse and looked past the bare, blowing oaks of the yard and across the fenced orchard grass of the pasture to the winding black county road, where any minute I expected my mother to arrive with Uncle Daniel.

"What has he ever brought this family except disgrace?" my father had asked earlier. Dad was an electrician at Lynchburg Coil and Armature, a large man with close-cropped, sandy hair who, though reared in the city, had always wanted to be a farmer. "No drinking, that's the first condition!"

"He's sick now, and John'll help," my mother had said, she a thin, erect woman whose hair and eyes were golden brown. She hadn't liked leaving Richmond for the country and was never at ease. Even when she was sitting, wheels raced inside her, her mind making lists of food or chores. Sleeping, she didn't draw up her knees but lay on her back, her arms and legs pushed down at attention.

I was John and hated having to help. I felt the shame and resented Uncle Daniel intruding himself into our lives.

I watched a vehicle speed along the road, a dark, muddy pickup driven by the Mastons, the family who owned the adjoining farm, a junk-littered, weed-twined hundred acres where hogs were raised and butchered. An east wind carried the stinking sourness of their sties, and on certain days you could hear the screams of hogs being put to the knife, causing my mother to close all the windows in our house.

My father had traded words with the Mastons over them not keeping up their part of the fence where our properties joined. As the rattling pickup curved away, a steely beer can thrown from a window glinted. Ditches were full of the Mastons' cans and other trash.

"He's two years younger, the baby of the family," my mother had said, speaking of Uncle Daniel.

I remembered him from Richmond, where he arrived with a young woman not his wife. He'd been drinking and wanted to stay the night at our house there, but my father wouldn't permit it. I peeked out an upstairs window to see Uncle Daniel standing in the drive, his arm around the slinky woman's waist, as leaves from the red maple fluttered about them. "Thanks one hell of a lot for the hospitality!" he shouted.

Yet he sent presents at Christmas—never much, a box of pralines, a book of animal photographs taken in Africa, a football helmet too large. Then gifts stopped, as had cards, letters, and phone calls from places like Mexico and Hawaii.

"But why now?" my father had asked. He paced in white wool socks over the square pink tiles of the kitchen and lifted his arms as if to receive a load dropped from heaven. Farm labor had hardened his body, and his skin was a weathered tan. He could toss a bale of hay to the wagon as easy as I shot a basket. That's when he was happiest, working around the place, sweaty, grain sticking to him, his big, rough hands reaching for weight.

"Just till arrangements can be made," my mother said at the sink. Uncle Daniel being her brother, she was cornered into defending him.

"He's not roosting here!" my father said.

The disgrace was that Uncle Daniel had been in prison. My father used the term *jailbird,* and my mother winced and lowered her face as if to pray.

Days were warm for late winter, the sunshine a clean glaze on the grass. We'd had snow, but it melted except in private places along the fence line and in ditches. Ice on the branch that ran through our pasture had thinned to laciness. Shaggy Angus cattle snoozed in quiet leas of the fields.

I saw the blue Dodge driven by my mother with hands set high and precisely on the steering wheel. Never in her life had she broken the speed limit or any other law, so how could she have a brother who was a jailbird? I ran down from the porch to open the aluminum gate across the dogwood lane.

Nervousness stiffened my mother, but Uncle Daniel sat smoking and smiling, a pale, balding man with a flattened nose and a chin so abrupt it appeared broken off. His smile turned up only the left corner of his mouth.

He lifted a hand to me as they passed. I closed the gate and ran after the car, but Mom was already out when I reached it. She'd opened the door for Uncle Daniel, who set a plaid cap on his head and gripped a heavy wooden cane between his legs. He dropped each foot to the ground and shoved his body weight over them. For an instant he swayed. He used the cane and the Dodge to steady himself as Mom grabbed for his arm. He wore a zipped-up orangy vinyl jacket instead of an overcoat. His pants were summer seersucker, his shoes unpolished black loafers.

"Shake your Uncle Daniel's hand," my mother said to me. I looked into eyes as light green as winter branch water, eyes too large for the thinness of his face. He held his cigarette loosely in the center of his lips, smoke drifting out around it. I felt the skeletal boniness of his fingers.

"You carry his bag," my mother said.

It was a canvas, olive-drab duffel bag, not a leather suitcase and not heavy. He wouldn't be staying long with so little. Our guest room was on the second floor, but Mom had fixed her sewing room on the first floor for Uncle Daniel. My father hadn't liked that either. We moved out her machine and patterns, and carried in a single bed, a chair, a table, a lamp. Uncle Daniel would use the lavatory down the hall and climb the steps for a bath.

As he stood looking at the room, an ash dropped from his cigarette

to the rose carpeting, and I saw my mother's alarm. She was glad my
father hadn't witnessed it. She hurried to the kitchen to bring a
seashell Uncle Daniel could use for an ashtray.

"I'd like a nap now," he said, and turned his whole body to my
mother like a person whose neck was locked. "Relax, Ruth, I'll not
disrupt the harmony of your household."

Yet he wasn't up in time for supper. My father drove home from
Lynchburg Coil at four, and during winter worked till dark around
the farm. He was used to eating at exactly six-thirty. He tried to be
patient, but his thick fingers flexed as if milking.

"Did you explain about meals?" he asked.

"He was so tired, the last one off the bus," my mother said. She'd
prepared a rib roast and anxiously watched the oven. "Bill, he used to
be a runner. My little brother won medals for running, yet he got off
the bus like a decrepit old man."

After supper we cleaned the kitchen and went to the den, where
Dad had built a fire in the Franklin stove. He didn't switch on the TV.
I studied my history, but we were all listening for Uncle Daniel.
Locust logs popped twice as loud as usual.

Finally my mother tiptoed to Uncle Daniel's room and peeped in.
She returned crying silently. I stood from the desk, and Dad swung
forward out of his recliner. We believed Uncle Daniel had died.

"He's still sleeping," Mom said, touching fingers to corners of her
eyes and drawing the tips down alongside her nose. "So terribly
tired. I remember how pretty he was. His hands are templed under
his cheek like a child's."

He wasn't up when I went to school in the morning, but that
afternoon he sat out of the wind on the front porch, his chair in the
sunshine. He wore the plaid cap, a clean pair of my father's white
cotton workgloves, and my father's old checkered overcoat.

"You a brilliant student?" he asked, his voice wheezy. He was
again smoking a cigarette. "I made Phi Beta Kappa at William and
Mary and was proclaimed a mathematical genius."

Before I answered, two shots cracked out from the ridge of the
rounded wooded hills behind the farm, .30-30s, and I hurried into

the house. My mother was practicing "Bringing in the Sheaves" on the upright parlor piano. She played for services at the Beautiful Plains Methodist Church. I asked had she heard the shots.

"Just you stay put!" she said, snatching her long fingers from the keys as if burned.

But that evening, when Dad came home and was throwing down hay for the stock, I told him. He walked fast to his Chevy pickup. He wouldn't let me come with him. I waited at the gate, and it was black dark before his headlights wound along the county road.

"They been up there," he said angrily. He meant the Mastons. "I found tire tracks."

Because Dad was upset, he became more irritated with Uncle Daniel smoking during the meal—not just at the end, but leaving a cigarette burning in the seashell beside his plate and putting down food to take puffs. My father hated smoking and pollution. He'd escaped the city to find clean air. He believed using cigarettes was the same as a man going out and seeking dirt to stuff down his lungs.

"It's ruining the flavor of my meal," my father said, waving a hand over his plate as if clearing fog. Again my mother was alarmed. "Can't you wait till coffee?"

Uncle Daniel smiled and snuffed out the cigarette in the seashell, but the smile was taunting, the way a person might react to the impertinence of a spoiled child. Mom dropped her fork.

After supper Uncle Daniel excused himself and went to his room, where he closed the door and probably smoked till he was blue. My father and I helped Mom in the kitchen. They talked in low voices.

"He just needs us while his papers are straightened out with the Veterans Administration," Mom said.

"What if they aren't?" my father asked, and my mother lifted her chin and turned her back on him.

Uncle Daniel had been told by his VA doctor he should exercise by taking walks, but he was so feeble and breathy he went only as far as the gate the first few days. Then he made it down to the county road. My mother stood watching at the dining-room window, her tense fingers holding back a gauzy white curtain she herself had sewed.

"He might fall in a ditch," she said.

So afternoons, when I stepped off the school bus, I walked with Uncle Daniel, moving slowly at his side along the road that snaked among hills still shy of greenness. Thawing had moistened the earth, and the south wind carried warm scents of new life, yet only the weeping willows near Highland Creek seemed to believe spring was close.

Walking tired Uncle Daniel greatly. Sweat formed on his temples, in creases of his face, and down loose skin of his neck. He'd take fifty steps, rest, and then try another fifty. Each afternoon he attempted to extend the distance. Though his wheezing was terrible, he didn't stop smoking as he raised his face to the sun.

He asked how old I was. When I told him fifteen, the left corner of his mouth lifted. He drew on his cigarette and whacked his cane against the soft bank. "I wasn't much older when I killed my first man," he said.

That night, after he was in his room, I asked not my father, who was working on the tractor out at the shed, but my mother. She knelt in the basement, scraping scabby whitish paint from a rocking chair she intended to refinish. Our basement smelled of earth, onions, Irish potatoes, dried apples, and the paint remover.

"It's his failing—he can't seem to help bending the truth," she said, pinching steel wool around slats and knobs. "He served in the Army, ran off from home to join, but never fought or went overseas. He was a corporal in the Signal Corps."

I didn't know whether he waited on the porch for me to come home from school because my mother asked him to or because he liked having me along. Even during warmer days he continued to wear my father's cotton gloves and overcoat. He swung his cane at weeds growing from ditches or poked gravel. He looked at water flowing under the one-lane iron bridge, the swiftness of Highland Creek. The Mastons drove by in a truck dropping smelly, manured straw bedding. The truck passed so close to Uncle Daniel it fanned his overcoat. He stared after it.

"They shot a cow—at least we think they did," I said, and told

Uncle Daniel how after the Christmas meal our first year on the farm my dad and I'd gone out in the pickup to drop bales of hay, which sank in the snow, and found the heifer on the ridge. "They were deer hunting. Dad posted the land, but the Mastons don't care beans for law."

They didn't care for much of anything, three bachelor brothers, all bearded and dark complected, living with their snuff-gumming mother in that ramshackle house surrounded by abandoned farm machinery and auto carcasses. Dad said at the Mastons' it was hard to tell which were the pigs and which the people.

"I'd have kicked ass from here to hell and back," Uncle Daniel said, a thing I told neither my mother nor my father.

Uncle Daniel napped as soon as we returned to the house, and would remain asleep till supper. He'd learned to be at meals on time, which helped with my father, as did restraint on cigarette smoking at the table. Mom and Uncle Daniel talked about a tree house they'd built among limbs of a sugar maple when children. Dad worked at being agreeable because he liked seeing my mother happy.

"You want to ask me something," Uncle Daniel said on Wednesday night after my parents drove to church meeting. We sat in the den warmed by the stove, the television on to a western movie, wind crackling the tin roof of the house. "You're dying to know why I was in prison. I'll satisfy your curiosity. I killed three men in a brawl."

He stood from Dad's recliner to lift his gray sweater and clean blue workshirt. The puckered scar resembled a track, one rail with ties, running aslant his doughy, swollen stomach. I hated looking at it.

"I threw two of them out a hotel window, and the third cut me from behind. He swallowed his own knife."

The scar convinced me this time he was telling the truth, and I wanted no more walks with him. I stayed at school long as I could, shooting baskets and spying on Anne Marie during cheerleader practice. When I reached home, I found chores, or hiked up to the hills and sat with my back against a locust stump to watch clouds carry Anne Marie's face over the sunny valley and shadow it, or to listen to wind playing the ridge with her happy voice.

My mother took me aside. She held my hands and forced me to

look into her encircling golden brown eyes. "What'd he do now?"
she asked, and wouldn't release my fingers. I told her about the three
men. I'd been seeing two of them tumbling through a spray of hotel
glass and arching to their deaths. I'd pictured the third man swallowing his own bloody knife.

Mom shook her head. "His failing again. No, he never hurt anyone, at least not physically. It involved money, not killings, when he
was a broker in Atlanta. The scar's from a prison operation for an
intestinal blockage. Now I need you to help me look after him. He's
not bad, just suffers from what our grandmother used to call a
runaway imagination."

I put on my windbreaker and John Deere cap to go after Uncle
Daniel. He was almost a quarter mile down the county road, the
farthest he'd gone, lifting his feet higher, and sometimes carrying his
cane instead of leaning weight on it.

"Was beginning to suspect you're a snob," he said, swerving his
wintergreen eyes at me. He reached into Dad's overcoat pocket for his
pack of Camels, shook cigarettes loose, and offered me one. I said no
thanks. "You never smoked?"

"Once and wanted to puke."

"What about girls? You think of those blessed little lovelies?"

I couldn't keep heat out of my face, the blood, and he laughed
himself into a coughing fit. I thought about Anne Marie most of the
time. She could be on the road or ceiling or in leaves of trees. I'd
picture her wearing blue gym shorts and shirt, her legs white and
slim, her red hair flying.

"Oh, I know the pain," Uncle Daniel said. "And the women who
have loved me, one a countess, an actual French countess I knew in
Atlanta, a woman so sleek she looked shellacked. She wore only silk,
always silk. She wanted to carry me back to France with her to live in
a three-hundred-year-old chateau that had a moat and swans."

Before I thought, I said, "You're lying." Then I believed he'd
jump me. Instead he whooped and wheezed.

"Sure I'm lying, yet not for money or to damage anybody. Good
lies are what we do to get by day to day. Think about it."

I thought about it. I guess he meant there wasn't much difference between dreams and lies, good ones, and I had plenty of those featuring Anne Marie. Anyhow, things were better for Uncle Daniel and me after that, as if we'd crossed a divide and understood the rules. I didn't mind walking and listening to his stories about life in Atlanta—the boats he owned, the plane, the horses. I stopped worrying whether they were fact. I tuned him out to think of Anne Marie.

We had a late snow as the land greened, trees budded, and forsythia flashed yellow. For three days I got out of school. My mother put me to work shining brass and her wedding silver. Uncle Daniel couldn't do anything around the farm, but he came from his room to help me at the kitchen table. He talked about the time he single-handed his 40-foot ketch across the Atlantic from Palm Beach to Le Havre. My mother gave me the look and smiled.

Uncle Daniel offered to set up books for our farm operation, but my father put him off. He was again worried Uncle Daniel might be settling in.

"It's more bureaucracy," my mother explained, keeping her voice low. "The VA misplaced his papers. He's called several times."

"I know he's called—I get the bills," my father said, nervous too about the farm and his job at Lynchburg Coil, where men were being laid off because of the business slowdown. "Can't he draw welfare?"

"Oh, please don't ask him to do that!"

"No, let him be genteel and sponge his living while my house smells of cigarettes, which I also pay for."

Snow melted, and warmth returned so quickly the land sighed, and all the gullies ran water. I heard the first peepers along the branch. Redbuds, dogwoods, and wild cherries bloomed. Uncle Daniel resumed his walks and liked me to name the leafing trees for him, ones he'd never learned in the city: hackberry, the Kentucky coffee, white ash, gum, Osage orange. He sat on the flaking railing of the rusty bridge and watched the stream flow under us, the water so clear that sunshine reflected off loaf-shaped stones on the bottom.

"Go ahead and ask," he said.

"Why'd you go to jail? I know you didn't kill anybody."

He eyed me, fiddled with his plaid cap, hesitated, and tapped his cane rapidly against the bridge, causing iron to clang. "Nothing remarkable. I worked for a financial house, and as I sat at my desk one summer afternoon I spotted a great opportunity. I was a chartist, a technical analyst, a person who makes investment decisions by putting his faith in numbers, and I saw what had to be a top in gold. You wouldn't understand, but the transactions involved promissory instruments called futures, and what I saw was that if I were able to borrow, not steal, some customer money that lay dormant in their accounts, have it just a few days, I could make a carload of dollars.

"And I was right about the top. At the end of the week, on Friday after the London opening, I was ahead close to a hundred thousand. I went to the Peachtree Club to celebrate, a believer in numbers, but while I was washing down my eggs Benedict with Bordeaux blanc, those numbers hadn't programmed in the paranoia of a Middle Eastern fanatic who sent his army against his cousin and neighbor in a dispute over a strip of sand so small you couldn't stick a beach umbrella into it. By the time I got back to my desk, gold was a raging fever, and I had a stack of margin calls higher than my hairline."

He frowned, squared his shoulders, and raised that broken-off chin. I saw another man in him, what he must've been once, sharp and dashing, like a magazine liquor ad, and the women had probably really loved him.

"It never felt like stealing," he said. "Even in my worst-case scenario I believed I could marshal the resources to pay the money back. But the media took that puny little war and made it seem the end of the world. It cost me my wife, my house, my reputation. Allow me to present you the distillation of my vast experience. In this universe there are no sure things, never ever, especially with numbers. And always sit near the door."

His skinny shoulders drew down as if he felt a cold wind. He started coughing and seemed to become smaller, grayer, wearier. Going home was slow, and when we entered the house, waiting on the hall radiator was a letter from the VA saying his claim for disability had been disallowed because his present condition could not be justified as service connected.

My father was on temporary layoff and what made him angry was how Uncle Daniel merely shrugged and dropped the letter into the wastebasket as if the rejection had no importance.

"You don't care?" my father asked, trying to keep from lifting his voice.

"The old government runaround," Uncle Daniel said. He sat in a straight chair at the kitchen table, and my mother stood behind him, her hands raised, though not touching him. "I can and intend to appeal. I'll hire a lawyer."

"Who pays for the lawyer?" my father asked.

Uncle Daniel exhaled slowly and worked to his feet. "Folks, I feel shame aplenty. If that's what you want, indeed I do."

He shuffled to his room, closed the door softly, and didn't come out for supper. My mother, so furious her stiffened fingers shook, seized plates from the table. My father, sorry and confused at his loss of control, escaped to the shed to work on the tractor.

Yet Uncle Daniel was waiting the next afternoon when the school bus let me off. Instead of Dad's old overcoat, he wore a ratty tweed jacket that must've been jammed into his duffel bag. We strolled the road to the bridge.

"I'll be leaving, but don't worry about me," he said. "I have this aunt, a rich old lady who lives in Arizona. She owns a ranch, raises thoroughbred horses, and has this emerald swimming pool right in the middle of the Painted Desert. For years she's been hounding me to come on out and help spend her money."

"Another lie," I said. "Mom would've told me if we had anybody like that in the family."

As the smile bent up the corner of his mouth, we heard a single shot from the ridge, the crack of the rifle a lash across the pale gilt greenness of the woods and new grass. Both Uncle Daniel and I jerked our faces toward the sound. It had to be the Maston brothers up there after another deer to grind up with their sausage to give it a wild tang. I knew the road they would take to come down.

"Hey, what's happening?" Uncle Daniel called after me as I ran.

I kept running till I came to the barbed-wire fence that lay along our property line. Just beyond was a field of copper broomstraw and a red dirt road that rain and winter had washed and eroded. A spiny gray gorse grew along ruts. I ran up between them.

I heard the Jeep before I saw it, the engine grinding down from the ridge in low gear. I could've squatted and hidden in broomstraw, though they were moving fast, the dark Jeep bouncing over stones. Big Clive Maston drove, he with his snarled black beard. His younger brother Calvin sat beside him, and it was Calvin who pointed at me.

Big Clive curved the Jeep through broomstraw and braked it beside me. I smelled oil and felt the engine heat. In the rear among tools, chains, and saws were the Winchester and a tawny speckled deer, its head lolling and showing a clean white throat that had been slashed and was still pumping blood. The hide seemed almost silverish in the sunlight. The deer had no rack, not even buttons.

"You waiting for the bus?" Big Clive asked. Calvin laughed.

"You all killed that doe out of season on our land," I said. I was trembling as I looked into Big Clive's eyes, tunnels into endless darkness.

"Doe, what doe?" he asked, and turned to Calvin, who spat over the side, the tobacco-juice blob landing close to my shoes. "You see any doe, brother?"

"He must've got a hard knock on his head," Calvin said. One of his eyes was widely out of orbit and freewheeling.

I moved a step backward into the wisping broomstraw and started down the slope, but Big Clive drove the Jeep ahead and looped in so I had to stop. He wore laced boots, grease-stained khakis, a netlike camouflage shirt with the sleeves rolled up around heavy biceps, and a camouflage hunting cap.

"Look, boy, we was just up the ridge hoping to find us a spring gobbler's tracks, and this crazy deer wouldn't let us be," he said as he gunned the engine. "Jumped right in the Jeep. What we supposed to do when a deer attacks?"

"We sure God got a right to defend ourselves," Calvin said. His large, crooked teeth were stained yellow-brown. I smelled pig farm.

A second time I backed away, walked around the Jeep, and moved down toward the county road. The Jeep cut through broomstraw to block me.

"So many deer running the ridges they bumping into each other," Big Clive said.

"Eat up a man's garden," Calvin said. "Who gonna miss one more deer?"

"Anyhow, he ain't going to tell on us," Big Clive said.

"Wouldn't be neighborly," Calvin said.

Those dark Maston eyes glinted at me like animals peering out of holes. I hated my fear. The doe still bled, her blood and black hooves glossy in the sun. I ran around the Jeep and down the slope, the broomstraw whipping my legs.

Uncle Daniel stood near the bottom. He'd started up the dirt road, hurrying as fast as he could on his cane. Sweat shined him, and he wheezed through his open mouth.

I heard the Jeep close behind me. They going to run me over, I thought. I saw my mother, father, and weeping Anne Marie at the funeral. As I reached Uncle Daniel, the Jeep skidded beside us.

The Mastons squinted. Calvin felt between the seats and brought up an unlabeled pint bottle of whiskey. He screwed off the top to drink, raw liquor and tobacco juice going down together. His stomach had to be the filthiest thing in the land. He handed the pint to Big Clive.

"You looking at something?" Calvin asked Uncle Daniel, that wild eye loose.

"Maybe he'd like a pull," Big Clive said. "Word is he used to be some terrible kind of drinking man hisself."

"I confess I have drunk a river in my time but never ever with trash," Uncle Daniel said.

I stopped breathing. Nobody talked to the Maston brothers that way, not even my father.

Big Clive peered at Uncle Daniel, who stood so erect I saw my mother in him, and reached to the rear of the Jeep for the Winchester .30-30. He settled it across his lap, drank from the pint, and swung the bottle back to Calvin.

"Crip, you reckon you could do a little dance for us?" Big Clive asked Uncle Daniel, and levered a shell into the chamber.

"I tell you, I gave up dancing a long while back," Uncle Daniel said. "Now you're upsetting me. I don't much care to look into the south end of a gun headed north, and I am politely requesting you put it down, stop pestering me and the boy, and get the hell out of here."

Big Clive lifted the Winchester, aimed, and fired. The bullet kicked up sod and red soil at the side of Uncle Daniel's left loafer. Calvin grinned as he screwed the cap on the pint.

"You grits think you can scare a sick man like me?" Uncle Daniel asked, and stepped toward the Jeep. "I've got carcinomatosis, cancer to you, and I'm going to be giving up the ghost any day now. I'd like to remind you the state of Virginia is again electrocuting men down Richmond way. You want juice, they'll provide it free of charge, no bill from the power company. Oh, it's a festive cookout, the meat sizzling, frying, splitting open, eyeballs popping. You shoot me, that's what you get. Any half-assed sheriff's deputy'll be able to trace it to you. Even if I fall dead on my own right here this minute, you're in for manslaughter. You boys better pamper me."

But Big Clive again raised his rifle. He closed one eye like a person taking unhurried target practice. When I wailed, Uncle Daniel waved me off.

"He won't shoot," Uncle Daniel said. "He laps up the rotgut, sure, but he doesn't care for the steaming juice they serve down in Richmond town."

Uncle Daniel lifted his right index finger and like a man plugging a leak laid it over the muzzle of the .30-30. Staring at Big Clive, he also breasted to the rifle.

"Here's your big chance for a ticket to the dandiest chicken fry of them all," Uncle Daniel said.

Slowly Big Clive pulled the rifle back.

"Now that's a lot friendlier," Uncle Daniel said. "You just hope and pray I reach home 'fore I die."

"Goddamn if he's. . . ." Calvin said, the eye madly roving. He hooked a booted leg from the Jeep.

"No!" Big Clive commanded Calvin without looking at him.
"But goddamn!"

"Haul your ass back in here!" Big Clive said, and shifted gears.

Calvin spat hard, cussed, and pulled himself into the Jeep. Big Clive set the Winchester at the hooves of the doe and again gunned the engine. He drove off fast, leaving a wake of bent and flattened broomstraw.

Uncle Daniel touched trembling fingertips to his face. He was exhausted. He staggered down to the county road but wouldn't let me hold him, though his mouth snapped for air. Coughing bucked him.

"Stop looking at me like that," he wheezed, half turned from me.

"You dying?" I asked, scared, shaky, my eyes wet and burning.

"Everybody's dying, and you mean you can't recognize a lie now when you hear it? I thought I taught you something about this world."

He couldn't make it all the way to the house. I left him sitting in sycamore shade at the side of the road and ran home for my mother and the Dodge. I didn't tell her what he'd done. I tried to act calm and said we'd just walked too far that afternoon. She helped him into the Dodge and the house, where he lay on his bed.

I waited for Dad, and when he came home I told him behind the barn. He fumed and raged and would've called the sheriff right then if it weren't for frightening Mom. She hollered out the back door to find what the conspiracy was about. Dad said we'd been discussing cattle to be culled for the spring auction.

Uncle Daniel hadn't come from his room, though Mom was ready to set food on the table. Nervous my father might again explode if he was made to eat late, she apologized and explained Uncle Daniel had overextended himself on his walk.

"Maybe I ought to see about him," my father said, and my mother's head came round from the stove like a person who heard trumpets and galloping horses. Dad had never made the offer before, or used that tone of voice.

Then we heard Uncle Daniel's door open, and in he walked. He appeared unsteady, white and waxy, but his head was up, his shoulders squared. He gripped the table's edge to sit.

My father hurried to position Uncle Daniel's chair for him, and started passing him food right after the blessing. My mother's hands became suspended over her lap, her eyes sliding swiftly from one to the other of us as if watching swallows dart about the barn.

When at the end of the meal Uncle Daniel sat back to reach for the Camels in his shirt pocket, my father leaned toward him and drew the book of matches from his thin, quivering fingers. Dad struck a match and lifted the flame to Uncle Daniel.

My mother was unable to hold it in any longer and stood, a hand flapping her paper napkin as if flagging down a train.

"I want to know!" she said.

But I knew whatever Uncle Daniel said or did, even the lies, I believed.

lover

"You're too old," she says, but I try to change her picture of me. I seek to be transformed before her sea-tinted eyes. Sixty-four is not old for a man who has been as carefully conditioned as I. Rare's the day I don't visit the company gym for a workout. During past years I won tennis trophies and once swam three miles across the Chesapeake Bay—from the Virginia shore near Stingray Point to a red buoy marking the Potomac channel. Sailors waved to me.

I don't forget Helen. I see her daily in misty passages of my mind. I drive through the arched gateway to the cemetery west of Richmond and stand at the foot of her grave, it, like the one alongside, level now to the sod. The third plot is mine, yet I no longer think of dying. I remember Helen's graceful fingers reaching across linens of the dinner table, the gloss of candlelight on her skin. I carry flowers of the season and set them by both tombstones, which themselves are like blooms in a field of frozen flowers.

I have my business, a manufacturing concern that produces controls for electrical appliances. Our first assembly line was little more than workbenches in a drafty shed, but now the buildings are sleekly modern, the interiors brightly painted and lighted. Employees wear laundered smocks and color-coded hard hats. We pipe music into offices.

My office is on the topmost floor, the window an expanse of thermopane providing a view over grass to the aluminum flagpole and sycamores along the James River. Each morning by 8:30 I arrive and look to the silverish green water flowing around chalky white rocks. Often gulls ride wind currents above the rapids.

I undertake the unpleasant chore of terminating a middle-aged employee caught carrying from the plant tools and parts hidden under his clothes. Spenser has been with the company twenty-six years, hired by me in our first expansion of the business following a public offering of stock. Personnel would do the firing quickly and coldly, but I have them send the man to my office, ask him to sit, and for a moment I chat of the old days when, shirt-sleeved, I often hurried along the line in an effort to expedite orders. Spenser will not meet my eye but looks at the bronze-colored carpet where his feet rest.

"Has anyone treated you unfairly?" I ask. He is whitely soft, the skin below his eye sockets spongy. I suspect he's a drinker. He no longer wears the company smock and appears alien. "We helped finance your home and loaned you money interest free to send your son to college."

"God I'm ashamed!" he says, and weeps. Like a woman, he drops his face to his palms and cries. Helen wept like that on learning of our son's death—David, who was flying fraternity brothers in the company plane to a Charlottesville football game. The Beechcraft struck the peak of a wooded mountain and pinwheeled burning into a gorge and river. I am sorry for Spenser, stand, and cross around my desk to lay fingers on his bowed back. I feel his pain.

"You won't be released," I say. "We'll allow you to make restitution. I do insist you undergo counseling."

My words cause new tears, and he wishes to embrace me, kiss my hand. I lead him to the door, where my secretary, Miss Baker, waits to escort him out.

"That's a very nice thing you did," she tells me.

I have watched Miss Baker. She is in her forties, a dark-eyed brunette with a girdled full figure. I have been attracted to her. She is clean, always lightly perfumed, and I feel the warmth of her body as she passes my desk. I've wanted to slide my hands over curves of her hips. I sense she would not object to a relationship properly pursued.

Late each afternoon I return alone to my house. I think of selling it as I steer my car between dogwoods and magnolias lining the blacktop drive. Various trees are diseased now, near death, and I should have them replaced by the nursery, but it was Helen who directed the landscaping of our home, and to take them away is also to carry off a part of her.

The three-story brick house has symmetrical wings and four flared chimneys. It sits on a knoll, and when I arrive evenings the windows appear lit. The light is a deception, just the sun's redness reflected in glass. The upstairs bedrooms go unused except for mine. Twice a week Lucinda, the cleaning woman, comes. The fountain has been shut off, the fish taken from the pool. Tendrils of creeper and honeysuckle snake through English boxwoods of the garden. Weeds grow from the tennis court.

I walk corridors and touch nothing, though I stand in my son David's room and conjure his last days at Washington and Lee. Snapshots of him and his sporty friends still line the mantel. I taught him to play tennis, but our trophies now are tarnished. In this room Lucinda is only to dust and vacuum.

Helen's room I stay out of altogether. She's been gone seven years, yet scents of her still lurk. After the funeral I left the running of the business to Carl Borman while I fled to Florida, where I intended to stay till winter seeped from Virginia, but at the end of four days I hurried back. Florida was unreal to me. Its dazzling colors, the restless beat of the ocean, disturbed me. The land and people appeared as flat and garish as postcard vistas for sale in hotel lobbies.

When I returned, my house was frigid. The oil furnace required thirty-six hours to draw coldness out of walls and furniture. I drove to downtown Richmond to talk with a real-estate agent named Gordon, who had done work for the company in acquiring acreage. He was enthusiastic about the listing, yet at the last minute, when he had an interested party in hand, I reneged on our agreement and sent him a check for his trouble.

I do not feel old. I keep fit, eat balanced meals, and avoid alcohol. My weight remains a constant 170. No fat hangs from me, and when I stand in the shower, water runs straight down the length of my body to my legs. I close my eyes slightly, squint and sight along those legs, and believe I am again young. I remember the shining eyes of girls.

I assume that for me love is dead. I live for the company, the increase of business, and I travel to romance design engineers and purchasing officers. I alone significantly widen our area of operations, though I never fly, not since David. I often feel more at peace in motels than at home. Motels provide warmth and light while my house has become a place of shadows no electricity will dispel.

When, therefore, I experience a surge of love, I am shocked. It is a spring day, the earth stirring. A veil of pollen falls from willows and yellow pines along the river and coats the water with a pale green film as fine as silk. Doves are calling. I leave work at 5:30 and stop by the supermarket in the shopping mall to buy a pittance of bread, meat, and milk. What I prepare I will eat standing.

The girl doesn't look at all like Helen except for her body's petiteness and a certain narrowness of face. Her skin is tanned and has the lovely sheen of youth. Her straight, blondish hair is carelessly arranged. She has a casual way of moving as if nothing in the world would hurry her.

Hands gripping the shopping cart, I stop and stare an instant before I catch myself and move on. By the time I reach the end of the aisle and the check-out, the girl is gone, and I feel I have lost something precious.

I wake during the night thinking of her. Ridiculous, but her face stays in my mind, a shimmering seen through darkness. She rises above my bed and beckons. "Forgive me," I say to Helen.

Each afternoon at 5:15 I drive to the supermarket, sit in my car, and watch the entrance. So many people, all concerned and harried, most appearing unhappy. To believe unhappiness is the natural order is easy. Life is injurious to one's health. I will not see her again. She was someone just passing through. I feel guilty and foolish, particularly when a company line foreman recognizes me and crosses the striped concrete to the car.

"Trouble, sir?" he asks. His name is Mills, and he wears mechanic's coveralls and a cap. I've heard he moonlights repairing automobiles in his garage. Fine. Ambition I understand and commend. "Waiting for a friend," I say, and thank him. As he walks away, I make a note to enter his act of courtesy in his personnel file. I worry that others are observing me. Distressed by my absurdity, I drive to the house, where fire reddens windows—again the evening sun's reflection.

An entire week I avoid the mall, but on Thursday I need groceries, and I see her. She wears a ruffled white blouse, tight jeans, and leather sandals. Around her brow is a red-white-and-blue hairband, on a wrist a jingling silver bracelet. Her hair is gaited to the easy rhythm of her walk. She appears bored, even petulant. I release my breath, realizing I've been holding it since sight of her.

I wait outside to watch her leave. She does not return to a car but carries a single paper sack through the parking lot to a sidewalk along a back street named Fern. I have never before shadowed anyone, tried to follow them while driving, and my slowness causes glares and honking horns. I consider passing her and waiting but am afraid she might turn off and be lost. She moves with her pelvis slightly advanced.

She strides across mowed grass fronting a small, white house with dark green trim at the windows. Behind it clothes hang from a line. She stoops, curves an arm under a calico cat on the porch, and lifts it to her face for a caress. The animal sways limply at her elbow. They go inside, the screen door slams, and I drive on.

A modest house, I am thinking, perhaps belonging to someone who works for me. Men's clothes are on the line—shirts, khakis, jockey shorts. The only female garment is a dangling white brassiere held by a clothespin.

At the end of the street I turn and come back to park in shade of a sugar maple. I am sweating but not from heat. My stomach flutters, my fingers shake. Are you crazy? I ask myself. Quickly I drive away and almost sideswipe a Pepsi-Cola truck.

Yet the next afternoon I'm back. I wait ninety minutes, and the girl doesn't appear. No life around the house. Doors and windows are closed on a warm May afternoon. No clothes hang from the line. No cat curls on the porch, furnished with a glider and two metal chairs. I think of the girl being squired by somebody else and am furious as if I have a right to her. A mother pushing her baby in a stroller peers at me. I drive away.

I work to forget. Work has been my salvation. I chair a quarterly directors' meeting and the spring sales conference. The company is opening another plant and introducing new products. We hold a convocation at the Hilton for the presentation of awards, then a banquet with speeches. The girl is almost absent from my mind.

Carl Borman, the organization's executive vice-president, looks into my office. He is my creation. I have chosen him to advance, groomed him, taught him to stand on the mountain for the long view. He wants my job. He craves it as he should, yet I find myself resenting him. He could mask the fever of his ambition.

"You must be tired," he says as if I'm already worn-out.

"Nothing's wrong with me. Whose wind breaks first when we run laps?"

"Hold it, Dave," he says. A meaty man of fifty-two with a touch of ruddy flamboyance, he laughs loudly and won't be insulted unless it suits him. "All I meant is you should slow down a little, maybe take another trip."

"Which of us is overweight?" I ask.

"Okay, I'm beating a retreat," he says, holding up his hands like a person dodging rocks thrown at him.

In truth, there are moments I feel dizzy and disoriented. I telephone Will Berry, my doctor, for a physical. He runs results of my electrocardiogram through his manicured fingers as if reading tape from a stock ticker.

"You have the heart of a much younger man," he says. "But watch your intake of salt."

What about my intake of love? I don't go back to Fern Street. I crowd the girl from my mind, occupying myself with hiring workmen to lime and fertilize my lawn, prune dead limbs, replace the sickly trees. Honeysuckle is dug up by the roots; the boxwoods are fed a mixture of nitrogen, cottonseed, and bone meal. I have the tennis court weeded, rolled, and relined. I twist the basement valve to the fountain, though I do not supply the pond around it with fish. Water sprays into sunlight and bends with breezes.

Yet nothing changes. I cannot escape the calendar and its reminders. I stand before Helen's portrait above the white marble mantle of the living room. She wears a simple dove gray dress, pearls, and earrings. Her aristocratic hands are folded over fluted organdy covering her knees. Between relaxed fingers she holds a pink rose.

"I have missed you," I say.

As I pace flagstones of the terrace and glance beyond the lawn toward the river, I am startled. I see Helen and David, he a child, both strolling through the last coral glow of evening, their shapes dusky in the fading light. They hold hands, circle, and sing. I want to shout. I clutch the stone railing and shake my head as if flinging off water. Of course it's not Helen or David but a young mother and her son who have wandered onto my property from the public park downstream.

The park is mottled, less than thirty acres, with a boat ramp and brown, wooden picnic tables arranged under willows. Children fly kites, and often I hear music and laughter. At nightfall, globed walkway lights reflect off dark, soughing water.

The problem is a break in the Cyclone fence along the boundary. Wind has blown limbs of a red oak across the fence and smashed it. I telephone the county administrator, and he promises to send his repairmen. I tack up a No Trespassing sign.

I am further angered by Carl Borman and the executive committee. Action has not been taken to raise the retirement age. I am the corporation's largest stockholder, yet I suspect plotting behind my back.

"We can buy their business for the inventory alone," Carl says, speaking of an acquisition prospect. He continues to upset me. His nature is to win over others at all cost, and I may have to find means to be rid of him, but will the board side with me any longer? "The real estate comes to us for nothing."

He slides a buttock over the edge of my desk, a familiarity I have never liked. Once I thought him a second son, but there is an ungracious force about him, a rude will my David never possessed. Through Helen, David had breeding and grace. At times he was sensitive as a girl. He once brought me a robin shot with his BB rifle, holding the stroked bird in his uplifted palms like an offering, expecting me to make it well. We dug a grave behind the flower garden, buried the robin in a linen napkin, and recited an awkward prayer.

"Books can be doctored," I tell Carl Borman. I want him off my desk.

"Sure, so I'll sharpen my pencil, fly to Tennessee, and cast a beady eye on their figures. Take along Hicks from accounting."

"No."

"Just like that, no?"

"Just like that. I built this company and am still running it!"

I have raised my voice, causing him to stand away and leave. I sit hot and confused. Carl has a marvelous feel for profit and dollars. What good would he be without ambition? I am tempted to call him back and apologize, but doing so might only confirm him in his belief that I am losing control.

Sundays are worst. I have never been religious in the orthodox sense. I did drive Helen to St. John's each week for morning services and myself took communion at the rail, but she was my religion. I saw God in the tender length of her fingers arranging a vase of flowers or in the swift smile lovingly shaping her face. When she left, God went too.

Sundays are the dismal emptiness of a cave where shapes dimly pass. I am surrounded by mists. The splash of the fountain is listlessly distant. I walk down to the river, only this time I step through the gap in the fence to follow winding paths of the park. Jays screech and flutter unseen among heavy tree foliage. A black youth, fingers snapping, carries a small radio, the speaker pressed against his ear. On shaded grass a girl drapes herself over a boy, who raises a knee and lowers his hands to her back.

A pair of tennis courts are located near the park's entrance, and, like my own till recently, they are not cared for properly. Nets are ragged, tufts of crabgrass flourish through cracks in the asphalt topping despite stompings, and lines have nearly faded, yet the courts are free to the public, first come first served, and often in use. People play now, call to each other, groan and laugh. Yellow balls arch and flash in dappled sunlight.

I stop as if struck. Ahead of me the girl sits on a green bench. She holds a racket, the head of which rests on the ground, the handle clamped between her bare, satiny legs. She wears a white tennis dress with a blue hem and collar. Her sweat socks are so short they rise just above her shoes. While she waits, she lifts her racket, backhands an imaginary ball, and frowns toward the park entrance.

I stand watching. My breathing is clipped, and I blot my hands against my fawn slacks. My guess is she's not with people on the courts but expecting somebody.

I move up silently and am able to approach closely before she realizes I am near. When she looks at me, I feel I have been shoved. Her aqua eyes are like the sea and so boldly direct I almost step back. Rather than paint or mascara, she presents the guileless beauty of youth. She wears a red terrycloth browband, and around her wrist is a silver bracelet. No rings on her fingers.

"The county ought to build more courts," I say.

She is, I think, not going to answer. She turns her eyes away, and her face firms impatiently. She will stand and walk off. I wish I'd given in months ago to an impulse to dye my hair black.

"A certain dirty rat named Tommy's not going to show," she says. She wishes to punish Tommy. The racket head bumps the ground. "You can never count on him except never to count on him."

"A shame when you've come all this distance," I say, and then fear she will wonder about my knowing how far she has traveled. Words spill from me. "Look, please don't think me forward, but I have a court at my place all lined and waiting. Just beyond the fence. I'd be happy to hit some with you. I've been hoping all day for a game."

Again she turns her solemn face up to me. I am smiling but feel exposed. Such a clumsy overture, and people on the courts are glancing at us.

"You live in the house with the fountain?" she asks.

"I do, and my court is very, very lonely. A terrible waste not to use it."

Is it disgust that hardens her expression? To control my trembling hands I stick them into my pockets.

"You're too old," she says, no graciousness or mercy whatsoever.

"I'm prematurely gray," I say, stung and flushed. "But I know the game of tennis and once played an exhibition with Don Budge."

"Who?" she asks, yet before I can explain or sell myself further, she stands. "All right. I need work on my backhand."

We walk side by side under willows, which are like fountains stilled. I will try to change her picture of me. I seek to be transformed before her eyes. Be calm, I caution myself, and think her blondish hair could use a brushing. Yet its lack of care and its freedom attract. I feel light of foot and find myself chattering about the day, the river, the Pekin ducks at the water's edge. An elderly couple are tossing torn bits of bread. They eye me, and I believe I know what they're thinking. I stare them down.

To the girl I say my name is Dave. She, offhand and matter-of-fact, tells me hers is Gail. She is used to giving her name to people. I slow to stay beside her, yet her stride is purposeful, no-nonsense, the way only females can move. Men never appear as busy no matter how important their errands.

We step through the gap in the fence, walk under a fringe of red oaks, and cross the lawn sloping upward to the house. The grass, the shrubs, the fountain are alive now that Gail observes them. Her pelvis pushes forward as she looks at things with open curiosity. She is impressed, and her eyelids lower slightly as if she's earnestly assessing the property's value.

We walk east of the house and past the sundial to the tennis court. How glad I am I ordered it worked on. When I open the gate for her, she smiles the first time. Lovely little teeth evenly spaced and wetted by her mouth.

"I need to change," I say. "Why don't you warm up on the backboard till I return."

I hurry into the house by the side entrance and climb steps. I haven't played for so long I'm unsure where my shoes are. I find them at the rear of my bedroom closet. The fabric and rubber are dry to my fingers, and I hope the shoes won't fall apart on my feet. I open and shut drawers in search of pants. They aren't in my room but at the bottom of a bureau on the gabled third floor, along with arid linens and tarnished silver napkin rings. I hear the thump of balls against the backboard.

No shorts for me. These are white ducks slightly yellowed. My legs are strong but veined. I don't want her to see them and again think of my age. I locate my Dunlop among pool cues in the game room. I still have dozens of balls, but they are so old that when I peel off can tops an ancient air escapes as if from the tomb.

"Let's use yours till I can lay in another supply," I tell her. She eyes the shoes and pants I wear. I suck in my stomach and brace my shoulders. Keep smiling, I tell myself. But what do I appear in her eyes, a grinning old fool from a distant century?

I'm so nervous I have difficulty seeing the ball. She plays aggressively, and her form demonstrates good coaching. She moves with the certainty of youth, no hesitation, no change of mind, but steps into shots using the full leverage of her slender body. She runs me around the court. Gradually my eyes focus, and the old timing returns. Lovingly I stroke the ball to her.

She spins her racket and wins the serve. She tosses hair out of her face, frowns, intent on beating me. She desires to hit each shot deep and reach command of the net. I rejoice in the sweep of her tan, muscled arms and the swivel of her lengthened body as she smashes an overhead. Her silver bracelet jingles.

More of my touch returns. I have always been judged an intelligent player, a placement artist. My stiff old Dunlop with its loose gut strings kisses the ball. I want her to look and feel good. I set her up for shots worthy of books.

"You going easy on me?" she asks after taking the set 6–2.

"Not me. I believe in winning."

During the second set I feel I'm expanding backwards into my youth. Movement invigorates me, the flight of balls, sunlight on her dress. I am careful to keep these games closer so she won't suspect I am painting a picture with her, using my racket as the brush. She wins the last point by stroking a backhand crosscourt, a maneuver that twirls her little skirt about her gathered thighs. I jog to the net to shake her small, strong hand.

"Super playing for your age," she says, wiping an arm over her mouth and across a cheek. She is panting.

I don't wince but explain about Don Budge: "He visited my high school and was kind to me during the exhibition, yet not too kind. A tall, skinny redhead who stressed taking the ball on the rise. Those balls hissed as if they had burning fuses attached."

She nods, not really interested, herself her own world, yet I love her for it and watch her remove the browband to squeeze sweat from it. Drops fall gleaming to the reddish clay. I'm tempted to reach out and catch them like gems.

As we leave the court, I ask whether she's interested in a cooling drink.

"All the way with OJ," she says, and pushes damp hair away from her neck so air will flow against her skin.

I'm glad I have orange juice. We enter the house through the rear, and she is again assessing value. I sense she's never seen a kitchen this size, with its stainless-steel counters, hotel range hood, butcher's block, and wall refrigerator large enough for men to walk into. She looks through the pantry and past cabinets of crystal to the dining room, where silver reflects in walnut of the hunt board.

"I'll show you the rest of the house," I say as I offer her the glass of OJ over ice cubes, and am moved by the delicate femininity of her wrist, it covered by a blond down on which are more tiny beads of sweat.

She sips while I lead her through the wainscoted dining room and under the hall chandelier to the living room, where the portrait of Helen hangs. She looks at the painting but asks nothing. She is more interested in the Chickering and depresses a middle C. The sound chimes long, like smoke drifting into other regions.

We inspect the solarium, attached by a glass-covered walkway to the domed greenhouse. The latter is empty of plants and flowers. They were Helen's as was the music, she who could play Debussy by candlelight while I sat in my wing chair and watched silhouettes of her fingers on the glinting keys.

"Orchids grew here," I say.

We climb the wine runner of the front steps to the game room, with its pool table, punching bag, outsized TV, and locked rack of guns, some of which I've never fired. Luther, our former houseman, comes twice a year to clean and oil them. Once in western Virginia I shot a buck but regretted the taking of such free, bounding spirit. Men said I got my blood sport from kills not in the woods but in the business arena.

I don't intend to show her my room, yet of her own she opens the door. The walls are sand-colored, and on them are pastels, Chesapeake Bay scenes collected and hung by Helen. Gail, however, is attracted to the bathroom, done in jade tile with a black sunken tub and a circular glass shower that shoots water at the bather from all angles. I reach inside to turn it on for her, and she laughs from the pink wetness of her mouth.

"If you'd like to try it, I'll find a towel."

"Well hardly," she says. She still carries her racket and balls, and the glass. Before I can stop her, she pushes on past to Helen's connecting room. Golden drapes are drawn so that only a jonquil twilight invades it. Gail reaches to the wall switch and stands staring. The pencil-post bed has a canary counterpane, and on the ivory dressing table with its triptych mirrors Helen's exotic bottles sparkle. Before the fireplace is a peacock fan.

"Wait!" I say to Gail, who opens louvered sliding doors to the closet where Helen's dresses hang. Out wafts a ghostly fragrance, still alive all this time in folds of her garments. I feel choked.

"The shoes!" Gail exclaims, and points. "You could start a store!"

She bends forward to touch a pair of gray pumps, and runs fingers up and down a black chiffon evening gown last worn at a Christmas ball of the Richmond Cotillion.

I no longer try to stop Gail. I feel peculiar, as if I'm being hurled at a great speed and shedding years in the wind. I lift the gown out on its pink, quilted hanger and hold it in front of Gail, along her body. She is much too slight for the dress, yet she partially shapes its cool fabric and laughs delightedly. I think of Helen the first time, not in this house at all but her small apartment, where, after an evening swim, I stripped the white-latex bathing suit from her warm body and we sank to the shag carpet to become one fervid flesh.

"Let's put it on you," I tell Gail as I hear the wind's roar.

"I don't want to."

"Of course you do."

"Hey, let me go!"

I must live it one last time—the youth and Helen, the hope, the promise of glory, the soaring. Gail struggles but finds I am indeed strong. She'll no longer think of me as old. She strikes with her tennis racket, but I knock it aside. Bereft of her little dress she appears frail, unblemished, childish.

I ride the wind. Her voice's harshness is replaced by distant cries. We lie on the golden carpet, and I draw her as if I can envelop and absorb her. Rushing of the wind subsides, my head lolls, and my ear against her chest hears the frantic beating of her heart. Her hands, fingers loosely curled, have dropped palms upward to the floor. They remind me of fallen birds and the robin David brought me to raise from the dead.

In the slowing whirl I begin to fear. I sit up and away but grip her wrist. I lift her torn tennis dress and attempt to cover her. It is not enough.

"I'll find you something," I tell her. Her eyes, though wet, are no longer sea-tinted but a small driven animal's. "Why don't you use that shower, and then we'll drive to your favorite store and buy you all the beautiful shoes and clothes you want."

I make the mistake of slackening my fingers. She is up screaming and running. I stumble after her through the bedroom doorway and down the steps. I am promising I won't hurt her, will do anything if she will stop.

"Please!" I call.

But she is out the front and racing across the lawn, holding that bit of dress as if it will clothe her adolescent body. Aware of my own nakedness, I slow at the fountain, hearing her cries as she flees to the fringe of red oaks and the gap in the fence.

I back toward the house. I need to clean myself. Blood is sticky on my face and elsewhere. I find her racket, browband, the spilled balls and silver bracelet. Charms hang from it—a banjo, top hat, piano, cat, a ballet slipper. When I am washed and dressed, I twist shut the basement valve that feeds water to the fountain.

I wait near the door. The wind is gone, the house again silent. They will come for me, yet no matter how I explain, they'll never believe what I have done is out of love.

faces at the window

The new minister was no boyish type, no limp, fair divine with eyes rolled heavenward as if drunk on God's grace. David Carson was built of muscle and bone, his height hardly more than Robenna's, not as much when she wore heels, his hair reddish brown and thick to shagginess. More than once she smelled the sourness of his sweat.

He came to Tobaccoton from the Virginia mountains, where his wife had died and left him two children to tend—a daughter, Ruth, five; a son, Paul, three. There was much debate among the congregation whether or not a minister lacking a wife should be considered, but after people heard David in the pulpit, they were strongly moved and voted without dissent to extend a call.

He stood above the great Bible, its page edges golden, its marker a wine strip of weighty velvet, and his strong fingers curled as if lifting. His face was nearly as broad at the chin as at the forehead. He looks, Robenna thought, more like a boxer or halfback than a pastor. Yet his voice wasn't particularly deep. Rather, the words came forth with a slow, gentle certainty, and that certainty gave authority even to such routine parts of the service as the announcements of hymns, circle meetings, and special offerings.

"Give thanks for your disappointments and failures," David preached. "Until you can praise God for everything which befalls, you don't understand the nature of faith."

After he moved into the manse, a black woman named Aunt

Lucille was hired to wash, keep house, and pick up in wake of the children. David himself did much of the cooking. He set his charcoal grill under high boughs of slim yellow pines in the backyard. He also strung a rope swing from a red-oak limb and was seen pushing two gleeful children out of greenish shade into sunlight. He drove them to church and allowed them to play around it while in his study he worked on sermons.

He made his congregational duty calls. To Robenna's he came on a Tuesday afternoon at 3:30, the chimes ringing her down from her room to the double door with its copper screening. The house had belonged to her father, a timber merchant and tobacco planter. Toward the end of his life, after Robenna's mother died, he built a place foolishly large for a man having only the one child—three brick stories with arched white porches all the way around the first two so that he or guests could walk from any room and look across the lawn toward the village or to the pasture, river, and weltering willows.

Robenna never talked about her father's mind at the end. She understood the yearning for grandeur in the small-town rural South. During another age he might have been a statesman or general, and often she thought of him mounted like those equestrian statues of gentlemanly warriors along Richmond's Monument Avenue.

She and the new preacher sat in her parlor among the family portraits, the grand piano, the Oriental carpets, and she offered him—he insisted she call him Dave—tea. She'd directed Hattie to shine the silver service especially for that.

They faced each other across the butler's table, both on blue Victorian settees that had belonged to her mother. Once Robenna considered selling or even giving them away, but now that Victorian was again in fashion, she was pleased she had not. She expressed her sympathy to the preacher—Dave—on his recent tragic loss.

"For nearly six years I had my wife Julie," he said. Like his hair, his eyes were reddish brown, and they were startlingly direct. "Even ten minutes of sharing a life with her would've made me a lucky man. I believe there is no random pain. All things, good and bad, work to a purpose. Would you kick me out if I drank a Coke instead of tea?"

He wasn't at all like old Dr. Pedden, who had been minister till brought low by Parkinson's disease. Dr. Pedden lay addled now in a Richmond convalescent home, his waxy face twisted and trembling. He had been an upright man in a different tradition of always wearing a suit in public, even when merely stepping outside to check the weather. He tipped his hat and bowed to the ladies. Had stiff collars been available, he would've worn one. For him to turn down tea offered by a member of his congregation was unthinkable.

Yet Robenna found herself not offended. Dave—she had to remind herself—had a talent for disarming people and getting his way without causing bad feelings. He was so casual, so offhand, you didn't realize you were being artfully manipulated. Before she emptied her Limoges cup and he his Coke, served in a highball glass chunked with ice, he had her agreeing to serve on the Missionary Board.

He drove about in a faded green station wagon and usually wore khaki shorts, a T-shirt, and a perforated, red-and-white billed cap. He worked around the manse, not only mowing grass, but also cutting honeysuckle from crape myrtles and pruning back japonica gone wild. He talked Sam Mayfield, a farmer member of the congregation, into plowing soil behind the house for a vegetable garden.

When Robenna passed on her way to the village, she might see Dave directing the children as they sowed seed while he broadcast fertilizer or leaned on his hoe handle. He waved to her as if she were one of the boys instead of Tobaccoton's first lady.

He played golf. No minister in memory, not even an Episcopalian, had done that. Between Tobaccoton and Lynchburg was the Falling River Country Club, where she on summer mornings liked to get in nine holes before the sun cooked off the night's freshness. She would then slip on a bathing suit, carry a magazine to the pool, and lie on a colorful webbed chaise beside the other girls.

"He has the swing of a pro," Carolyn Taylor said as she massaged suntan oil into her shaved calves.

"Very physical," Toots Bonnert said, her body shaded to her hips by the tasseled yellow sombrero she wore. "Wish he'd swing my way."

"Toots!" Robenna said.

"Now, Robenna, don't have a stroke," Toots said. "Ministers are men too, the beautiful rats."

Robenna drove to the club a bit late on a Wednesday morning in June and wasn't able to find a foursome. The day was so shimmeringly clean after a thundershower she hated returning home without a game. She decided to play a ball against herself. She hired Billy Bo from the caddy house to carry her bag, Falling River being one of the few courses remaining that hadn't given way to carts. Billy Bo was a small, shiny black boy who in his life had never lost a ball and would wiggle down a groundhog hole to earn the dollar tip she always handed him.

At the third tee stood the preacher, Dave. The third was the most difficult on the course because a hundred yards off the tee ran a branch where rushes grew and snakes slithered—copperhead moccasins, their slick, bumpy skins glimmering in sunlight slanting among pine boughs. A caddy had been bitten.

Dave appeared sporty in tan shirt and slacks. He wore a white cap level to his eyes. His brown golf shoes were scuffed, though polished. He flexed his driver before bending forward to punch his wooden tee into turf.

As he addressed the ball, he worked his feet to set his spikes, gazed over the branch, and started his backswing with a hike of a hip. At the top he paused, rotated downward with easy grace, and applied no power through his wrists till he reached the hitting area. The ball clicked and whooshed away. His follow-through carried him over onto the side of his left foot.

The ball, an inverted arc, rose as if it would fly forever. From the top of its trajectory it tailed off into a slight hook that bounced into a roll along the fairway's contour. Billy Bo widened his plum-colored eyes. Robenna estimated the distance at close to three hundred yards. When Dave turned to pick up his tee, he saw her and grinned over those impossibly strong and attractive male teeth.

"Like to play along, lady?" he asked.

"Not after seeing what you just did to that ball," she said.

"Luckiest shot of my life. Glad somebody was around to witness it."

She walked the soft, needle-strewn path to the women's tee. Usually when she drove, she was able to see the name on the ball, Titlest, or at least the indentations, but this morning her eyes would not focus, and she felt tense. As a result, she shanked her shot, causing it to slice away and bound into rushes. Her face heated up. It was the same old business with men.

"Got it marked," Billy Bo called, and was probably thinking snake.

"I haven't done that in years," she said to the preacher.

"Cut down on your backswing," he said. "It's making your club head loop at the top."

He stepped to her side, took the driver from her fingers, and demonstrated the shortened swing. She'd had lessons before, many dollars worth, but he made her feel a beginner. She glimpsed the tan shirt pulled taut across his broad back, saw the strength in his neck, the gathered power in his legs, and suddenly was nauseous.

"I have to leave," she said, and Billy Bo looked at her.

"Hey, what'd I do?" the preacher asked.

"Something I forgot," she said, and left. He caught up with her and walked partway to the clubhouse, trying to convince her to continue play, but she wouldn't turn back. After paying Billy Bo, she drove home without her usual shower or visit to the pool. In the dim, close hush of her pink bedroom she sat at her dressing table and stared at herself. She thought she was over that. She had believed it completely.

The mirror made a frame around her dark eyes peering from dusk. She was still a pretty woman in the classic manner, like porcelain she considered herself, fine imported china. Her hair was black, her face thin but not too much so, rather what might be termed delicate and well-bred. She had worried about the length of her neck till she learned people, like the girls at Agnes Scott, judged her to be a landed aristocratic Virginian.

So had her husband, Whitt. Princess he called her and brought her pearls—but she wouldn't think of that. She had erected a wall past which he was never allowed. Sometimes, however, during the languor of early morning he slipped over the wall and tormented her with memory before she could defend herself.

That afternoon she recovered behind the house among flowers of the garden. Her salvation was fingers digging into rich black soil. Since she sold off side acreage to Uncle Henry Pellem, who disappointed her by developing the land into tiny lots for sale to mill people, she had sheltered her yard with luxuriant American boxwoods, the largest in the area. No green was greener.

Need had not compelled her to release the land to Uncle Henry— the trust her father left was sizable enough to cause the Richmond bank to send a young man twice a year to humor her. She had given over the land simply because a family member requested it. Later a boozy, weeping Uncle Henry had begged forgiveness as he confessed his deceit.

She didn't merely grow flowers. She used tulips, verbena, lupine, and other blooms to form designs of fleurs-de-lis, clock faces, and peacock fans. She, like Toots Bonnert, owned a sombrero, which she wore, together with gloves that had flaring yellow cuffs. Chap, her black man, toted away the discarded pickings for a compost heap behind the white board-and-batten tool shed.

Sweaty herself and smudged from work, she yelped when the preacher came around the house. He still wore golf clothes except he'd changed his spiked shoes for leather moccasins crushed at the heel. She realized her hands fluttered like a maiden's attempting to cover flesh.

"Before I entered the ministry I used to be a coach and am in the habit of telling everybody how to do things," he said. "I apologize for ruining your morning on the links."

She protested he most certainly had not and escaped into the house. She hurried upstairs, where she closed her bedroom door and actually pressed her back against it as if he were attempting to force entrance. Damn him for popping up places! He was much too familiar. Nobody called at her house without notice. Didn't he understand women never liked being surprised?

Yet his ministry pleased her. In particular, he was having great success with the church youth. Their attendance had shrunk while Dr. Pedden stood in the pulpit. Dave led a group on a canoe trip down Falling River, where they rode rapids and swung out on a vine from a birch tree to drop into the swift water. He started a drive to collect aluminum cans from county drainage ditches, the proceeds from their sale to be donated to a fund for sending underprivileged children to summer camp.

The pews filled, and receipts went over budget. Dave used anecdotes in his sermons, amusing stories of his days in the Army, and even when he became serious his messages were persuasive in a friendly, conversational manner, more like a man chatting on a corner with his buddies than a divine high up the mountain handing down God's thunderous commandments.

"The Lord will forgive all except you love not," Dave said, and seemed to be speaking to Robenna personally.

She hesitated about having him to a meal. The custom was for each member of the congregation to invite the preacher at least once, but then every minister until Dave had also brought a wife. Robenna worried an invitation on her part might not appear correct in the community's eyes.

She decided a luncheon would be acceptable, on her screened-in porch overlooking the garden. Bees swarmed around blooms, the ruby-throated hummingbirds sped to mimosas, and in the boxwoods doves cooed lovingly and long. Her Hattie would do the cooking, and Chap, wearing his white jacket and black bowtie, could serve.

More silver was polished, and she chose a menu of tomato aspic, backfin crab meat on iceberg lettuce, and a chocolate éclair. She wavered about wine but had heard from Toots Bonnert at poolside that Dave had been seen drinking beer with members of the men's team after a softball game. Robenna concluded he would not disapprove of her serving the wine, and he himself could always turn his glass upside down.

He didn't understand the occasion's semiformality. Instead of jacket and tie, he wore shorts—the khaki spotted from his painting the church steeple—a soccer shirt, the perforated cap, and the same crushed moccasins. His arms and legs were fuzzy with reddish brown hair. Around his thick wrist was a cheap digital watch, the plastic kind people buy at grocery stores or cut-rate drugs, but somehow he gave it dash.

When he saw she had on a rose chiffon gown, hose, and heels, he didn't act embarrassed or make excuses but laughed over those strong teeth. He eyed the table set with linen, crystal, and silver.

"I thought it was for a sandwich," he said.

"It's my fault, I should have been more specific," she said, though she didn't feel it was her fault at all.

"One thing, the food won't care how we're dressed," he said.

She couldn't stay peeved. He was a hungry man, and his maleness made her luncheon seem too feminine, too bridge clubbish. No doubt he preferred slabs of beef or drippy barbecued ribs, though she never ate that heavily herself. He didn't refuse the chilled Johannisberg Riesling but drank it negligently, as if it were there merely to quench thirst and not to add charm and subtlety to the meal.

Yet he was not coarse, just healthy and so full of vigor. She guessed his age to be close to hers, somewhat shy of forty. When he finished the éclair, he leaned back and actually thumped his stomach like a tom-tom.

"I usually smoke a cigarette after a meal," she said, restraining a smile.

"If you won't tell anybody, I'll join you," he said, and accepted one of her Virginia Slims.

It was so pleasant sitting in the purplish shade of the porch, the slight breeze carrying fragrances of the garden. He noticed her work with flowers, her art, really, and stood at the screen to look at the fleurs-de-lis, clock faces, and peacock fans. He questioned her about varieties, and she named them for him: African daisies, Sweet William, Oriental poppies, coral bells, heliotrope, and snapdragons.

She glanced down his back, the slope of strength to his waist, all that dominant yet gentled masculinity. For the first time in years she felt no uneasiness at being alone with a man. Her reaction surprised and scared her a little.

That night on her bed she heard the mockingbird in the crape myrtle and watched the sheen of moonlight cross her sheer white summer curtains. Though hot and moist, she hadn't switched on the house's air conditioning. Rather, she shed her nightgown and lay naked, feeling the pale blue satin sheets beneath her. She didn't touch herself—she would never do that—but she burned with temptation and believed she felt the moon glaze pass over her as lightly as breath. Rigid, nearly choking, she resisted her body's urge to thrust upward into it.

A second time she met him at the Falling River Country Club, and on this occasion she did play golf with him, able to control herself sufficiently to post a respectable score. Though she used the women's tees, he outdrove her mercilessly, but close to the greens she recaptured strokes, largely because she hit her balls carefully and he boldly. Her putts on the last two holes dropped in.

"Glad I didn't put my money down," Dave said, pushing his cap high on his forehead.

"You gamble with members of your congregation?" she teased.

"I don't consider a little wager a mortal sin," he said. "I once won eight hundred dollars in a poker game aboard a troop ship, and a corporal pulled his .45 on me. Just like the Old West. The next afternoon I lost the money shooting dice. God doesn't punish us for our humanity but only to shape us. Pain is the potter's wheel."

No doubt he'd been a worldly man. From conversations she gathered he'd joined the Army right out of high school, fought in Vietnam, and after his discharge sold office equipment and coached at a military academy before going off to college and the seminary. He married late, a young legal secretary in Bluefield. She died early one winter evening when the car she drove skidded on an icy bridge and flipped over the railing into a rushing mountain river so cold its spray froze on jutting rocks of the gorge.

"That pain was the toughest to transform into God's concern," he said. "I believe it was a test."

"Of what?" she asked.

"My acceptance of Him as the master craftsman."

She discovered he was fond of horses. She still owned Whisper, the last of a string from days when she rode the circuit. She had also hunted with the Deep Run hounds, but Whisper, a blazed chestnut gelding, was aged now, and dressing herself of late to mount hardly seemed worth the effort.

Dave drove his children to the farm, the one large piece of property remaining that had belonged to her father. She leased it to be planted in tobacco on shares. The two-story white frame house was lived in by a family named Arnette, who looked after Whisper, painted the stable, and repaired the fences. Summers they supplied Robenna with fresh vegetables, and each winter they brought her a smoked ham.

She had Chap clean and oil a saddle for Dave, and watched him ride his children around the paddock. He was a natural horseman. The place to see it was in his hands. Through the fingers, she had read, the soul of a noble animal and its rider join. Dave's were strong, yet kind, and as he urged Whisper into a reluctant canter amid shouts of happiness from the children, Robenna thought of those hands on herself and blushed as if she'd been caught in a shameful act.

The same afternoon, when she returned to her house and shuffled through mail in the silver tray on the hall table, she found of all things a letter from Whitt, her ex-husband. Her grip loosened on the envelope as if it would blister her skin. She didn't want even to open it. She carried it to her walnut escritoire and slit it. Whitt wrote he would be passing through Tobaccoton on his way to a lawyers' conference in Charlottesville. He asked permission to stop by and say hello.

She sat immediately to write she saw no good in that, nothing to be gained by either of them. She sent Chap with the letter to catch the five-o'clock mail. Still she felt Whitt had again entered the house, that she might meet him around every corner. She found herself locking doors early.

How could one so wellbred and handsome be so depraved? Perversion had not marked him outwardly, yet within Whitt a coiled serpent curled and rose in darkness. The terrible things he required of her. Even today she would not sleep in that bedroom but used another at the rear of the house. During the weeks after her divorce when she suffered a breakdown and agreed to therapy at the private Richmond clinic, she was unable to put words to Whitt's acts, though prompted by a kindly old doctor. Some things a lady could never admit to, and she above all else considered herself a lady.

Dave drove out two or three times a week to groom and ride Whisper, and at summer's end, when the Virginia State Fair held its Horsemen's Classic, she felt it not improper to invite him. Each year whether she attended or not, she subscribed to a box. His boisterous enthusiasm amused her, especially in the timed jump-off, which Rodney Jenkins won with a demonstration of corner cutting and daring as exciting as any sport alive. Dave and his children leaned over the railing to cheer.

She suspected people in Tobaccoton were talking, and that bothered her. She walked into her kitchen, where Hattie beat biscuits in a gray earthen bowl at the counter. Robenna sat at the round cherry table to smoke a cigarette. She and Hattie had been together too long to pretend.

"He a pretty man all right," Hattie said, flour up to her elbows, like evening gloves. Robenna had been able to get her into an ample white uniform but never into decent shoes. Hattie wore loose carpet slippers that scraped lazily around the house. "They asking him to work with the Rebels." The Rebels were the high-school team. "Tell me he can kick a ball from here to Danville."

"Hattie, do you think Tobaccoton would be scandalized out of its mind if I invite him to the Fall Cotillion?"

"Might could. Take me. I never seen a preacher dance."

Robenna believed she'd be able to get away with it, not only because she was old family, but also because Dave was so popular. Oh, the biddies might fuss, yet they weren't capable of doing her any lasting damage. So, hands stickily moist and trembling slightly, she phoned him at the manse.

"I'm obliged to warn you the dance will require a costume," she said, and felt short of breath as she waited for his answer.

"I always wanted to be Daniel Boone and kill me a bear," he said.

She spent the morning of the dance under a hot dryer at Jenette's La Mode, Tobaccoton's beauty parlor. Plump Jenette wanted to blondine a streak through Robenna's hair.

"Why, I'd never do that!" Robenna exclaimed, causing laughter to rise from the other cubicles.

She'd arranged for her costume with Sally Denton, a local seamstress whose husband Wayne had been crippled under a John Deere tractor years earlier. Robenna would use the Little Red Riding Hood outfit only once, yet bought silk for the skirt, cape, and cap. With it she wore a white off-the-shoulder blouse. The skirt was pinched to her small waist, pleated, and raised almost to her knees. She chose also crimson nylons and black patent-leather pumps. She had shapely legs, though spare, and the costume was quite sexy, even shocking.

She and Hattie helped piece together Dave's costume using bits of old clothes and a suede cap Hattie sewed a squirrel's tail onto. Robenna provided a Civil War musket from her father's previously undisturbed gun collection, and when Dave, wearing his fringed chamois jacket, brown corduroy pants, and the moccasins, walked up the front steps to call for her, she thought he indeed resembled a pioneer, a man who would push into wilderness and survive bears and Indians. She imagined him clearing land and chinking a cabin around which children clad in homespun played.

In a wicker basket Chap gilded for her, she carried copper-colored mums from her garden to hand out to friends and admirers at the club. Those she had aplenty moving through the joyous swirl of the ballroom, with its French windows, glitzy balloons, and whirling color wheel. People made over her. Never since her Richmond debut had so many males asked her to dance. She even flirted a little, believing it would make her more attractive to Dave. Other women vied for him, especially Toots Bonnert, got up like a saloon dance-hall girl.

Nobody resented Dave's being present. He drank the fish house punch like everybody else. Men laid their arms fondly on his shoulders or leaned to him to laugh. She loved the warm pressure of his hand on her back. She wasn't sure whether her light-headedness was a result of the punch or his nearness.

During the last dance, the chandelier dimmed, the color wheel spun slowly, and balloons glimmered down like red and yellow blossoms. Though aware of the length of Dave's body, she didn't draw away as she had with other men. She slid her cheek against his and believed, as the spectrum striped them, that she felt his lips move briefly to her hair in the gentlest of kisses.

She didn't care whether or not people noticed. Let them think what they wished. She clung to his arm as they left the clubhouse, and when he drove her home in his station wagon messy with children's toys, she sat close. She'd already decided to invite him in. The night was warm, smelling of leaves, many of which had turned and flashed brilliantly in the headlights. She wished it were cooler so she could strike a match to the fire Chap had laid.

She poured them each a Chartreuse, adjusted the hi-fi, and joined him on one of the Victorian settees. She had touched up her lipstick and freshened her perfume. His legs were stretched out, his moccasined feet slewed, a contented man.

"I owe the baby-sitter a fortune," he said when the grandfather clock in the front hall chimed 1:30.

"Let me pay, Dave. You're my guest."

"No deal, lady. When I take a dame out, I do it right."

She drew her legs up between them on the settee, the mesh of her hose catching a glaze from the table lamp with its painted globe. She possessed aristocratic ankles. Her father had told her that. Dave, like men at the dance, eyed them. Her off-the-shoulder blouse slipped lower across her breasts.

She thought of this man who had again brought her alive, this combination of the spiritual and earthy. Might she be a minister's wife? Once the idea would have seemed ridiculous, but now she felt she could do anything at his side. She wondered whether the pain and humiliation of her marriage to Whitt had been a way of molding and preparing her for this moment. God, the master potter, at work.

She smiled at Dave, dropped a shoulder, and shifted so that her nylons rasped, her silk rustled. She willed him to lean to her, caress and kiss her. She wanted him to have the aching fullness of her breasts.

He blinked, yawned, and wiggled his toes. He talked of a church basketball league and wondered whether local schools would permit use of their gyms—as if at this instant that were important.

"Let us have no violations of church-and-state hassles," he said. "Listen, I got to think about placing these tired old feet on the path."

She moistened her lips and left them parted. As she offered to furnish uniforms for the church team, she hoped her dark eyes caught a gleam from the lamp. He kept talking and gathered himself to stand. She stopped his words in midsentence by bending to him and kissing his mouth. His fingers slid along her hip and waist to her shoulder and neck. She lowered her head to nip at a single chamois fringe of his jacket.

"Are we getting a little bit too het up here?" he asked.

She took him by the hand and drew him upstairs to her perfumed bedroom. The pale blue satin sheets glistened in rosy light so dim it hardly cast grasping shadows on the pink walls.

When at the stroke of three he slipped from the bed to dress and leave, he once again kissed her. She stood naked at the window of the upstairs front hall, knees bent, arms crossed over her breasts, to watch him lope stealthily across the dark grass toward his station wagon. The noise of its starting was explosive in the serene ebb and flow of the murmuring night. She pictured heads rising from pillows to listen, eyes rubbed from sleep to peer past curtains fingered aside.

Would he come back? For a moment she was seized by shame and terror. Then, as she returned to her bed, she felt a calming strength. Staring upward into darkness she was barely able to make out the rounded shape of the ceiling light. A wheel, she thought, and spread herself as if again accepting him—as if accepting everything.

"Shape me."

She spoke the words twice and dropped into sleep. When she woke at dawn, she was turned to the window. She watched the sun pierce the oak leaves and creep along the sill. She just might call La Mode later and allow Jenette to streak her hair with gold.

moorings

The young couple unsettled families who were born and raised on the harbor even before we spoke. The couple talked funny and wore clothes that clashed with the pearly, weathered wood of our docks and pilings—striped shirts, red-and-yellow shorts, and blue-billed caps which had crossed golden anchors, though neither knew the first thing about earning and holding a master's ticket.

From Norfolk they came, he—according to Ed Horsley, who trucked iced crab meat to the city—owner of a fancy restaurant fixed up in an old ship's chandlery, three stories decorated with palms, parrots, and rickety ceiling fans that made the place like the South Seas. They hadn't cleaned the gull-crusted outside of the building, so when a person walked in he felt he was leaving a dingy world of warehouses, grime, and broken bricks, and entering the dome of a gilt paradise.

"Could be they nice enough," my husband Jess said—he back from the bay, the Chesapeake, in Virginia, not Maryland.

"They not been living here long enough to have nice," I said. I was Josie, Josie Catlett, and my fingers were cut so bad from shucking oysters that dishwater stung them till I danced at my sink.

The young couple wont our people, not just clothes or tongue. Our men earned bread for the table by tending crab pots, tonging oysters, or hauling from pound nets fish that flipped over on and slapped their rubber boots. Women worked in the cannery or wherever they could. Dollars came hard and slow, and when we spent them, our hands lingered long on the coin.

The young couple, whose last name was so different I didn't even try to remember it, used money like it didn't have to be counted. They bought five acres of waterfront on a wooded point jutting into the harbor, and hardly argued with Wesley Hudgins over the price. Their Norfolk architect hired local labor at wages fifty cents to a dollar higher than the going rate. Just about every man who worked the water signed on to put up the house, leaving us women to caulk boats, mend nets, and bait the first crab pots of spring.

The couple's new house rose fast above the longleaf pines, a series of wooden, slablike towers set at angles to one another, those slabs golden in the sunshine. Stained-glass windows reflected the evening light. Salt-treated decking circled different levels, and on the highest was a platform with a flagstaff. We believed the house would tip over during the first nor'easter.

"I'd as soon ride out a blow in a chicken coop," Jess said.

Nights the couple switched on every bulb in the house so it looked like a cruise ship crossing dark water. Music sounding over the harbor disturbed great blue herons used to sneaking in on slow-flopping wings to raid crab pounds. I tossed in my bed hearing drinking, dancing, carousing.

"I'll rub your back," Jess said, though I hadn't complained aloud. He'd felt the pique in my body, the stiffness. His thick fingers were gentle over my shoulders and down my spine, their scaly roughness pleasing to my skin.

"We like music but don't force it on nobody," I said. "You see what they swim in, or rather what she don't?"

For along with the house the young couple had built a pool, or had it built. They never lifted a hammer or saw themselves, unlike Jess and I, who poured the concrete footings of our bungalow. The pool didn't use salt water from the harbor but drew fresh from a special well drilled just to supply it. The water was lit by lights under the surface that colored the darkness above like the glimmering blue bubble of a Portuguese man-of-war.

"Spare they bathing suits is all right," Jess said. With the other men, he'd been working at the house.

"Stuff hers in a thimble with room left over," I said.

During the summer the young couple drove up weekends with guests. They did some shopping at our market in Great Marsh, but mostly they brought their meat and bread from the city. The wife was a tall, thin blonde whose short hair was messy as a bird's nest. Her stomach's flatness told she'd never born no children. Her skin was satiny tan, and she painted her fingernails and toenails purple. She laughed too loud and snapped her fingers as if hearing music when there wasn't none—only the cries of gulls and ospreys spiraling above the dock. Louise Pruitt, who ran the market at Great Marsh, said the young woman bought and smoked little cigars.

"Doesn't anybody around here have maids?" the young woman asked.

She found a black woman to work for her, Minnie Mahan, and dressed her up in a green-and-white uniform to wait the table and clean the kitchen. Minnie's son Moss was also paid to tend bar at parties, he in a white jacket and black bowtie bought just for him. Each Sunday Minnie carried enough tote home to feed her family into Thursday. She quit her job at the shucking house, and most of the week sat around on her porch drinking pitchers of iced tea and playing cards with her deaf mother.

"You been discovered," I said to Jess at dinner. I'd cooked him fillets of a flounder he'd brought in from his crab run. "That's what Minnie's telling. Here all along I thought we knew who and where we was."

"They can keep discovering me as long as they pay what they been," Jess said. He was not only a waterman, but also a plumber, shipwright, and carpenter. He'd nailed up cedar siding on the couple's house that didn't have any front or back, just glass sliding doors everywheres.

"They think we're hicks and dumb," I said.

"We're part hick, you got to admit."

"We're what we chose to be. Nobody's invited them here to judge."

Jess and I almost left the harbor right after we married. He had a chance to live down in Newport News and work as an apprentice in the shipyard, but I was growing big with Aubrey, our son, who's now a seaman second-class in the Navy. We put off leaving, and then we put it off some more. Finally we forgot we'd ever planned to go.

"They pull your nose or something?" Jess asked. He was thirty-nine, a year older than me, a raw, handsome man broad in the chest and face, his hair still black, his chin blunt as a fist. Lots of girls chased Jess before I tripped him. He was so strong he could tighten his fingers over clams and twist the shells open. He'd do it down at the dock to show off.

"I can see them thinking," I said.

"Now, Josie," Jess said, smiling, his teeth so good he'd never in his life had to visit a dentist, his eyes gray as unpainted planking. "Even you can't see nobody thinking."

"I can smell thinking," I said.

The woman was too thin in her tight pants and peekaboo blouses. The man appeared short next to her, his skin fair, his small hands clean and unmarked as a maiden's. His red hair was longer than her blond. He seemed more boy than man, and when he came to the dock to buy hard crabs or a sack of oysters, people smelled a sweet scent and eyed each other.

"God, I love it!" he said, standing at the edge of the dock and looking out across the harbor to the white sand of the spit that separated us from the bay. Ospreys banked and cried above wind-twisted cedars, terns dived and splashed, and jumping mullets broke the glittering surface. In shallows around the green marsh, gulls and black skimmers rested, along with herons who stood as erect as stakes marking oyster shore. The young man lifted his hands palms upwards. "Do you all realize what you have here?"

"Sho," Jimmy Callis, who worked pilot on a scallop boat, said. "We got mosquitoes, jellyfish, salt water seeping into our wells, and holes in our roads and bank accounts."

The young couple bought a sloop as out of place on the harbor as a lily among weeds. Ours were rust-stained, dead-rise workboats built by hand and passed from fathers to sons. Wind had long been given up by men who farmed the waters. They'd gone to Evinrudes and Mercury outboards, and all our boats stank of fish, oysters, and crabs, as did the men themselves when they came home in their caked rubber boots and shell-splattered overalls. To us a boat was a living. To the couple it was a toy.

They christened the sloop *Wavy Dancer*, though local men named their boats after their wives. My Jess's was the *Miss Josie*. *Wavy Dancer* wasn't honest white but pale blue like skim milk, the sails too. Colored pennants flew from shrouds, chrome stanchions and pulpits flashed, and nylon lines were so shiny they reflected sunlight. Each time *Wavy Dancer* ran in or out of the harbor she shamed us.

"Don't they have a right to spend their money the way they want?" Jess asked. He was washing up in the bathroom, his shirt off, his arms and back muscling when he raised his hands to lather his face and neck. His waist was still a young man's. "Who they hurting anyhow?"

"Who they helping?" I asked.

"Me and you they helping. They lay their money down, and if they want to run around the harbor playing sailor, I don't give a damn as long as they checks don't bounce from the bank to my pocketbook."

The men liked to stand on the dock and watch the young woman, who laughed, called their names, flirted. If she ever used a brassiere, it didn't do much for holding her in. She wasn't really skinny but close, and wore makeup and bright scarfs over her bird-nest hair. She did smoke dark little cigars, clamped them right in the center of her teeth, and the men hollered and kidded her. They offered her a chaw, which she turned down, again laughing, winking, and snapping her fingers.

When *Wavy Dancer* ran aground at low tide in the mud south of the channel, all the men raced over in their boats to help. Instead of being upset, she and her husband made a party out of it, switching on the music and handing cold beer over the stern. I stood on shore seeing through binoculars. Cans glinted in the sunshine, and it sounded like the Fourth of July celebration at the VFW. The couple made a party out of everything.

"They don't understand how serious the bay can be," I said to Jess that evening while he cleaned and gapped the plugs on his old Evinrude, which had been kicking off at low throttle.

"They don't understand how serious anything can be," he said. "Hell, Josie, they just children."

I thought of our son Aubrey in the Navy all the way to the Pacific Ocean. He'd not got much chance for fun but had growed up helping Jess. Aubrey was a man before his years because on the harbor there was nothing else to be. Scrape bottoms, plant oysters, and sharpen stakes for pound nets was his day after school. Never time to go out for the baseball team, and when he graduated, he had to leave home to find his dollars where he could.

"But it don't seem fair they can play from dawn to dark while everyone else works," I said.

"Well, it's a free country and don't you go turning into no radical on me," Jess said.

The young woman drove to our house on a Saturday afternoon while Jess and I worked picking squash, butterbeans, and sweet peppers. Her tires crackled on our oyster-shell road. She parked her Jeep in pine shade, the Jeep the same skim-milk blue as the glossy hull of *Wavy Dancer*.

She wore a denim jacket and pants, a wine jersey, little ceramic earrings, silver bracelets, rings on her fingers, hose, and black high-heels. The legs of her jeans were cut to her slimness, and the jacket was fashioned short and not meant to be buttoned. Heels, jewelry, slinky denims—a sinful flaunt to honest, hard-working men and women!

She began chattering even before she was in talking distance. She raved over my blooming verbena, Shasta daisies, and scarlet sage, and at the same time was lighting a cigarette, not a cigar, and using her hands as she spoke like a person leading a band. She knelt to and o-o-oed over our dog, Tom, who was half black Lab and the rest everything else in Wyndor County. Tom could retrieve a mallard, scaup, or pintail without getting a lick of spit on the feathers.

"Look at him's eyes, oh such pretty golden eyes they are, yes, some beautiful eyes this baby here has!" she said. Her kneeling drew her pants even tighter around her legs and hips, and her wine jersey pulled up to show a strip of skin not roughened by salt spray or honed by wind but sleek and creamy. It was skin kept in a velvet box. We didn't own a phone, and she'd come to get Jess to help find a leak in *Wavy Dancer*.

"We could run her up to Crisfield and have her hauled, but it'd take weeks the yard's so busy," she said. "Can you spare a minute to peek at her? We'd be eternally grateful and delighted to pay."

"Won't hurt none to look, I guess," Jess said. He was eying her like all the men did, though pretending not to. He knew I was watching.

"Well super terrifica then!" she said as she straightened up and pulled down her jersey over the strip of coddled skin. Words kept coming from her painted mouth, speeding over her perfect little teeth. Her shoulders braced to push out those breasts too big for her thinness. Her silver bracelets jangled, and she flicked her cigarette onto our lawn.

"Just any time it's convenient," she said, and stepped away on those heels so high and sharp they sank into our grass, her hips swinging above her long legs and silky ankles. She snapped her fingers and left behind whiffs of perfume.

"What's wrong now?" Jess asked, turning to me as she drove off.

"Did I say anything was wrong?"

"You're thinking it."

"You're thinking I'm thinking it."

"Josie, long as they passing out money like it was plentiful as greenhead flies, we might as well grab a handful. I need me a new outboard."

"Eternally grateful and delighted to pay!" I said. "Just keep your eyes on your business."

He drove the pickup over to *Wavy Dancer*, which was now moored at the new private dock in front of the couple's house. He told me they were having themselves a sunbath in the pool, lazing around on floats when there wasn't enough minutes in the day for anybody else to finish his work. Jess had to ring a brass ship's bell screwed to the cedar bathhouse to stir them.

The couple led him down to *Wavy Dancer*, the boat not good honest planking like my father went to sea on, but fiberglass, chemical stuff they popped out of machines like plastic toys. Which was what *Wavy Dancer* was, with frilly little blue curtains at the windows, and in the cockpit red pillows decorated by white stitching shaped like anchors and sea horses, and music, always music coming from someplace in the rigging or down in the companionway. Boats was never meant to have music.

Jess lowered himself through a lazarette to the bilge and found water right enough, though the fair, smiling young man said he'd pumped her only that morning. Jess checked the stuffing box and all the through-hull fittings before he found a hose clamp on the cooling intake that needed tightening. Took him five minutes.

"So piddling I didn't want to charge," he said. "They kept pushing money on me. So here, go buy yourself a hat."

And he handed me a new twenty-dollar bill.

"Did the woman have her top off or on?" I asked.

"She wore a bathing suit and so did he. They matched."

"He had on a woman's bathing suit?"

"Well hell no, but the same material, kind of slick zebra stripes."

"Remember, Jess, I was pretty once too."

"Baby, what makes you say that when you still beautiful enough to make movies?" he asked, and rubbed fingers over my cheek, but that was all, no hug or kiss.

They called on him for more work. If they had problems with their well pump or TV antenna, they came in the Jeep to get Jess over with his wrenches. They hired him to build a shed to store a lawn mower and garden tools.

"What they need either for when they'll never use them?" I asked.

"They got to have them for somebody else to use."

"Might as well rent a room you over there so much."

"You been noticing our bank account lately?" he asked. I knew he worried about the falling price of crabs, so many in the harbor they threatened to crawl and clack over the land. I held my tongue.

I too was pretty once, slight, with dark brown hair and eyes, and I owned nice clothes—a white silk dress, a matching hat with ribbons, and white shoes. Plenty of harbor boys came knocking at my door, yet I set my cap for Jess, who brought me a half-melted British gold piece he dredged up while patent tonging for clams. A history teacher at the high school figured the coin was from an English ship that had burned during the Revolutionary War.

Jess sailed the couple in *Wavy Dancer* because before we married he worked the deep bay out of a skipjack, using it to tend his pots in the far water. Like his father he grew up knowing wind, and when he came back from *Wavy Dancer*, he'd laugh at mistakes the couple made—jibing, heading too high, and Freddy, the young man, forgetting to make the line fast to a cleat before lowering the anchor, and losing it.

"Call him Freddy now, do you?" I asked.

"It's his name, what you want me to call him, Abraham, Isaac, and Jacob? All he thought you have to do is point the bow any direction you'd like to go. Got in irons every time he come about. I taught him to gather way, run up, and backwind the jib. He's going to be all right, though, he's smart enough."

"They pay you for that too?"

"They pay for everything."

"She wear clothes on the boat or go half-naked?"

"Come on, Josie."

"What I am, the way I look, I got that way with you," I said.

"Hold it a second. You accusing me of something?"

"I think they charming you."

"And I think I'm going to have me a new Evinrude."

After Jess finished the shed behind the house and stained it, the couple wanted electricity run to their dock. Jess dug a trench, laid the wire, and connected up the all-weather light mounted on top a creosoted piling. Nights when I was restless, I'd sit on the side of the bed and see the light burning over there, a pale yellow streak on dark, still water. They'd forget to switch it off, and often it'd be burning during the daytime too.

"They consider us quaint," I said to Jess as he sorted crabs from his boat into bushel baskets on the dock. The crabs were tangled and came up in wiggling, snapping strings.

"Consider us what?" Jess asked.

"Quaint is what Minnie Mahan heard them call us."

"What does *quaint* mean exactly?"

"Peculiar is what it means."

"Could be we are to people not raised on the harbor," he said, and tossed a squirming, speckled young terrapin that crabs had been pinching back into the water.

"They say we talk funny."

"What about them talking funny? Ever hear anybody pronounce *shallot* or *gunnel* the way they do? I had to ask twice."

"They laugh about us."

"We laugh about them."

"I don't do much laughing lately in case you hadn't noticed," I said.

"I noticed all right. If you was to laugh hard, it might scare me half to death."

"You giving me much to laugh about?"

"Much as you been giving me," he answered. He slid the bushel baskets into the back of the pickup and slammed the tailgate. When Jess got mad, he seemed to grow, like all his muscle and flesh expanded, like bread rising. His gray eyes fired up. That anger made me feel I was being blowed back by wind. He drove off and stayed out late drinking at Donk's Place, where men sat on crates in back among heaps of oyster shells. I didn't question him when, smelling of wine, he lay down beside me in the dark. I was thinking I had nowheres to go.

For a cut, wash, and set, I drove the truck to the beauty parlor in Bloxom. I couldn't afford silver bracelets, but I bought a red dress, nail polish, and a pair of sheer dawn nylons. On Friday, when Jess came in from the bay, I was painted, perfumed, and decked out church-go-to-meeting. Jess whistled and walked around me. We ate a restaurant meal, necked through the drive-in movie, and afterwards loved it up long and hot. Yet I couldn't shuck oysters or pick crab meat all day and stay pretty and sweet for Jess too. Lots of times I just got tired.

"Josie, would you like to learn to swim?" he asked. He was still working over at the young couple's place.

"Me do what?"

"They found out I can't swim. They asked how come I been living on the water all my life and didn't. I told them nobody around the harbor ever swam. They couldn't believe it and offered to teach both you and me. Claire says she'll get right in the pool with us."

"You call her Claire?"

"Don't start that—Claire's her name."

"Who needs to swim except people what don't work?"

"Just give me a simple answer, would you like to learn or not?"

I thought of myself in a bathing suit. I wouldn't look anything like the thin young woman Claire. My hips had got wide, my thighs thick. It'd only make her appear all the better.

"I'd sink to the bottom," I said. "But thank Claire for me."

"I'll do that thing," he said, not caring to notice how I'd used her first name.

He bought a bathing suit, the first he'd owned in his life, yet didn't keep it home, which meant it must have hung over in their bath-house. I thought of him taking off his clothes and feeling air on his bare skin. Jess seemed to become handsomer every year while I settled into myself. I was dumpy was what I was. Maybe I should've gone with him anyways, but I stayed in my kitchen putting up jars of corn, beans, and cowpeas for the winter.

When Jess wasn't learning to swim, he worked building a brick entranceway at the head of the pine-shadowed lane leading to the couple's house. They wanted a gate they could lock during times they weren't home. I walked to see Minnie Mahan early Wednesday afternoon while she sat on her porch playing cards with her mother.

The mother was gray like garden soil, and the toes of her tennis shoes just tapped the floor from her chair. Despite the August heat she drew a white shawl around her pinched shoulders. On a table was a pitcher of iced tea with half a lemon floating in it. Minnie waddled away to get me a glass. She wore a loose, pink cotton dress and orange flipflops. The mother kept cocking her head as if hearing something in the distance, though she was deaf as rocks.

"I don't know as how I ought to be telling," Minnie said, sitting in her squeaking wicker chair and spreading. She flapped a funeral-parlor Jesus fan in front of a round, sweaty face blacker than pine pitch.

"I always been fair to you," I told her. "I never treated you better nor worse than anybody else around the harbor."

"Miss Josie, I don't see nothing terrible. They has parties, dances, and drinks a river, but I ain't saw anything I had to close my eyes on, especially about Mr. Jess. They like him to sing for them."

"Sing what?"

" 'Bout the fisherman and the shark."

I knew the song, one Jess learned from his father, and his father from his before that. It was called "The Smiling Shark."

> Said the shark to the fisherman,
> Come in and swim with me.
> Said the fisherman to the shark,
> I think that can hardly be.
>
> Said the shark to the fisherman,
> I'll show you gold of the deep.
> Said the fisherman to the shark,
> My bones I prefer to keep.

The song went on that way verse after verse till the shark finally tricked the fisherman into the water and made a meal of him. Jess used to sing the story when Aubrey was a boy, but he had done no singing for us of late.

I didn't say anything at supper, and I stayed quiet afterwards while Jess put his stocking feet up on the hassock to watch TV. He was restless. He reached for his pipe, scratched his scalp, poked at his ear. He walked out and stood on the screen porch. He lifted his chin as if trying to catch a breeze, but I believed he was looking at lights over at the young couple's house.

"They using you," I said behind him.

"How they doing that, Josie?"

"They make you sing for them and laugh when you're not there."

"Nobody makes me sing what I don't want. If I sing, it's 'cause I like singing. And if they using me, I like that too. They happy people, I got money now to buy me a new outboard, and when they want to use me some more, I'll sing till the crows complain."

We didn't talk much. He got up from the bed, ate his sausages and biscuits, and went to the bay to tend his pots. I finished my picking and canning. The TV never seemed to shut off.

Crickets began sounding the end of summer as green faded from reeds and marsh grass. Still the young couple had parties, every light on in the house, the stained-glass windows glowing like beacons. Across the water I heard music and laughter, and I believed I heard Jess too—loud and long. I pictured him singing and dancing over there. I thought of him holding the tall, slim woman, Claire, whose fair, smiling little husband likely wasn't much man.

When Jess slipped into bed beside me, I listened to him breathing. I slid my hand over to his and touched his curled fingers, but he pretended to be asleep. I heard the rising tide lap the shore.

Heat of summer lingered in the bay. Way past frost the days stalled warm, the water holding the sunlight. Crabs swum down to the sea and worked themselves into mud to wait out the winter. Men brought in their pots and took to oystering or the scallop boats. Jess cut and split firewood to stack beside the porch.

The young couple didn't visit their house so much, which stayed dark nights, though *Wavy Dancer* was still moored at the new dock, her shadow lying across ruffled, moonlit water. Maybe they won't come back, I thought.

Jess tried to make my birthday nice. He bought me a winter coat, and we drove to Maryland for a steak dinner. I'd already got a package from Aubrey, a barefoot Hawaiian doll wearing a hula skirt. I set it on the mantel. Jess loved me that night, but it wasn't the same. He was both inside me and far away.

The couple came back in late November. They wanted Jess to

winterize their house and sail *Wavy Dancer* up the coast to Bay Haven, where the marina would outhaul her and set her on blocks.

"How you get back from there?" I asked.

"We phone Minnie, and she sends Moss after us in the Jeep."

I watched *Wavy Dancer* slide out of the harbor. The day was sunny, fifty-five degrees, wind from the southwest at ten knots. The boat seemed a flat shape against the copper marsh, and gulls spun above her mast, their whiteness flashing in the clean light.

Through binoculars I saw Jess at the wheel, the woman standing beside him. She wore bright green slacks and a red windbreaker. I didn't spot her husband, who could've been down below. As I watched, she took off Jess's work cap and set her own on him, a yellow one with a long bill. She adjusted the cap on his head.

After they were beyond the sandspit, I watched the sky. The breeze stilled, and they had to be using their engine. I thought of them out in the sunshine on quiet water, eating a sandwich, drinking beer, hearing music.

Then the light changed as if a hand passed over the sky. I knew how quick everything could turn on the bay. Before you were able to shut your door, wind might back and blow from the north. The sky became purply brown and shredded, and chop churned up from the sea bottom. The radio broadcasted gale warnings.

Rain hissed in fast and hard, slanting like steel wire. Blowing pines bent before it as boats bucked at their moorings. Gulls and seabirds gathered in lee of the marsh, their feathers lifting along their hunched bodies. I lit a fire in the stove and stood at the window.

He's going to die, I thought. She'll kill him in her yellow cap. Wind would push them down the bay and out to the ocean. I fastened on my raincoat and walked to Cousin Adam Clegg's house to make a long-distance call. The Coast Guard at Bay Haven had received distress signals, yet none from *Wavy Dancer*.

Jess would be too proud to admit he needed help on the water. He'd drive a boat into the deep before he'd shoot up a flare or radio a Mayday. I counted out money for the call and walked home through the rain.

After dark I sat waiting by the fire. Wind played a howling tune on the flue, but rain slackened to scattered drops that sounded like buckshot throwed against the roof. The wind veered and dropped, and when I stood on the porch I heard the horn at Gate Shoal Light, though I couldn't see past a milky mist that hid the spit and harbor mouth.

At three in the morning headlights skimmed the wet windows. I ran out, but it wasn't Jess. Instead Cousin Adam's boots splashed through puddles as rain ticked his black slicker. He wrapped arms around me.

"The woman's in the hospital," he said. "Rescue pumped water out of her. Wait a second now. Jess could still be found. They looking."

The Coast Guard came on him floating, his hair caught in and his head bumping the black leg of a channel marker. Unlike the woman he wore no life jacket. That was Jess. His swimming lessons hadn't been much help.

Aubrey got an emergency leave and flew home from the Pacific. We buried Jess on a Sunday afternoon. As we stood by the grave, a southern breeze fanned whispering reeds, and silent, rain-washed gulls rode it like swells.

indian gift

So easy it was for Calvin. He had, people said, a talent, a gift, a magic wrist, which when drawing back the fly rod sensed the waxed green line's straightening behind him and flattening on air, then rolled it forward to uncurl and serve up the black-and-white popping bug with a soft plunk and gentle twitch exactly under branches of the drooping willows. Doc Dupee, who Calvin sometimes brought fishing, told him he should have been a surgeon.

For sure he was no surgeon or even a tooth doctor, but he could sneak away evenings from the farm's weary rows that stretched into the fiery sun like a road to forever. He first shifted his eyes toward the house to see whether Loris was watching. He stored his fishing gear not at the house—narrow, two-story frame with a brick chimney at each end—but in his tool shed. He'd slip behind the hay barn and wind down the soft, shaded path among loblollies to the pond.

Not that he tried to fool Loris. He hoped to spare her fretting. She had no itch to escape her house. That woman could drop a mule working, though she was hardly five feet tall and her arms were tiny as a girl's. She watched every penny with magnet eyes except she ordered the phone put in so Wesley could call from Charlottesville.

"He don't have real friends up there," she said.

"If he needs help, he can call Puckett's Store," Calvin said. The store was down the road at Five Forks, an orange cinder-block building that had a red tin overhang and two rusting gasoline pumps.

"When they open, but supposing Wesley needs us in the night?"
Calvin smoothly drew back the rod tip for another cast to the
willows. He sat in the stern of a wooden johnboat built by his own
hands. Loris worried herself skinny about Wesley being away at
college—God almighty, at the University of Virginia, where snotty,
high-toned boys drove foreign cars filled with licked-pretty girls to
dance on the lawn! Sometimes Calvin and Loris just stared at each
other across the kitchen table, stunned by the miracle of it.

Truth was they had a bad time deciding if Wesley should go. It was
opportunity, they saw that, but also temptation. In Charlottesville
students drank hard, shot dope, and fornicated. All the colleges did,
you could read it in the papers and see it on TV.

"Wesley's strong in the faith," Preacher Sneed said, wearing no
tie and exposing the wattle of his throat. Calvin and Loris had driven
over to see him at the parsonage, a white cottage next to a small,
spired church beside the highway to Danville. He reminded Calvin of
a turkey, like the gobbler from the pine woods that got himself
trapped in the sanctuary and scared Miss Bonnie Watkins, the organ-
ist come to practice, cross-eyed. "That boy's stanch. You could go
bear hunting with him."

"We could use him too," Calvin said, thinking of those long rows,
the dark tobacco that needed suckering under the blistering sun, the
dryness of dust in his throat which blackened his spit, the sweat
burning his eyes like battery acid.

"He deserves his chance," Preacher Sneed said. "The Lord has
opened a door."

Lying in bed nights Loris argued both sides of it. Calvin would
doze off and wake to hear her mumbling, using her words and his,
both asking and answering the questions. It wasn't necessary for him
to speak at all. Loris knew him so well she reached into his head and
picked thoughts out like taking peanuts from a jar.

"I'll sew for people," she said. Pause. "And I can plant extra
tatters and a watermelon patch." That last was her speaking for
Calvin and exactly what was in his mind.

With a paring knife she sharpened her yellow pencil and set the lined pad on the kitchen table to figure money. The university offered a grant-in-aid because Wesley had a strong arm and a fast ball that whacked a catcher's mitt like a heifer's hoofs cracking against planks of the barn. Calvin knew his stock, and Wesley had gotten the best from him and Loris—not so tall, but strong and steady, capable of lifting, yet light of foot, his hair a barley brown like Calvin's, his eyes water green like Loris' or the pond during coolness of evening.

"It'll pinch," Loris said. "But think of Wesley walking like a millionaire's son under those white columns."

Wesley did well up in Charlottesville, took to his work, and pitched good ball through the spring and also during the summer league down in Tennessee. Calvin missed him on the farm, realizing how big a load the boy had taken off him these past years. Calvin didn't begrudge it a second, and his extra aches and tireder bones were just reminders of the good that had happened to his son.

Crops were bad. First too wet a season, then the rain quit as if it would never fall again, the sky white, the red soil split like a cracked clay pot. His tobacco grew a thick, coarse leaf. As he worked his rows, Calvin thought of the pond, it still blessedly full, and the great bass which might bust up out of the green calm like a highballing locomotive. In his mind his magic wrist played the fish as if using rod and line to draw pretty pictures.

During Thanksgiving vacation his second year away, Wesley caught a ride home and trudged up the lane carrying his suitcase. He usually moved with a full stride, his arms swinging, his eyes raised, but that afternoon he poked along and looked down as if searching for a lost dollar. The boy was seeing his mind on the ground, and Calvin knew something terrible bad had happened at the university.

Loris planned to feed Wesley till he begged for mercy, but he hardly ate. She cut her eyes to Calvin. While she cleaned the kitchen, Calvin walked the boy to the barn to throw down hay for the stock, who, huddled out of the wind, butted and bumped each other for position. Pines were blowing and bending southward.

"I saw him pull up a sleeve and take it from his arm," Wesley said, explaining the honor code and the pledge he'd signed. Yet he'd not turned in the other student, also a ballplayer, who ate at his training table. "I keep thinking of his folks. I know it'd kill you and Mom if I got kicked out for cheating."

"You do what you promised," Calvin said, proud, thinking, we brought him up right, Loris and me. "Everybody pays for wrong. Your fellow's better off learning that now than later."

When Wesley returned home at Christmas, he would say only that his teammate had left without speaking to anybody. The following Sunday Wesley gave witness at the church, standing beside the pulpit and telling other young people in the congregation how he came to Jesus. "I had the best examples in the world. No person who breathes air was ever born to finer parents, and I thank the Lord for them." Loris, her eyes wet, squeezed Calvin's rough fingers.

A second summer Wesley rode the bus to Tennessee to play ball. All he got for it was expenses and a chance to be seen by scouts. He hit so well the coach put him in right field most of the time instead of pitching. Once a week, every Monday, he wrote a postcard home.

But, God, it was hot and dry. Doc Dupee phoned to go fishing, he white-haired and half-crippled by swollen knees, yet he'd still make house calls in the middle of the night. Calvin rowed him around the pond. Doc just couldn't seem to catch fish while with his first cast Calvin hooked a three-and-a-half pounder that curved his rod tip beneath the water.

"You ought to go tournament," Doc said, and it became a dream for Calvin, part anyway, the rest being Wesley making it in the big leagues, and seeing him on TV or both Calvin and Loris sitting in the grandstand and watching Wesley smoke that fast ball past batters who swung so hard and missed they wound up like pieces of twine.

Out on the tractor, when Calvin was running his rows and swallowing red dust, he was able to think of the two things at the same time, Wesley winning a big one and himself away from scours, pigweed, and tobacco worms as he floated on a greenness of water that had no limits, a pond as big as the ocean and sudsing with fish. He saw himself shaking hands with Wesley, both champions, each happy in his pride and respect for the other.

On the farm nothing went right. Crop prices dropped below costs, and the sky forgot how to rain. Even if he wanted to fish for a living like the pros, he had to have money and equipment. You needed either to be rich already or to win the backing of a sporting-goods company. He thought of writing those companies, getting Loris to pen it for him pretty. The names and addresses were in the barber shop's *Field and Stream*. What stopped him was his picture of poor men all over the world doing the same. And Loris might've laughed.

Then the damn John Deere broke down, the transmission making a racket like rocks rattling in a bucket. He winched the tractor up on the truck to carry it to Tobaccoton in the morning. Worrying, he struggled for sleep. Bound to be one hell of a bill.

"Don't use profanity in this house," Loris said beside him in the dark.

"Hell ain't much profanity," he said, not sure he'd spoken the word. Again she must've reached into his mind.

"Enough to tip the balance," she said, and he pictured the Lord picking up men by the tail like mice and weighing them on moral scales before lifting some into paradise and tossing the rest into the eternally burning pit.

It wasn't just the John Deere and the poorness of prices and crops. Wesley needed books, clothes to wear under the white columns, and living-on money. He was studying engineering, which was hard for a boy who graduated from a country high school. What Wesley learned, he held onto forever, yet he had to rassle to pull it in. They didn't want him fretting about money. He might up and quit to return home and help if he suspected they were sacrificing.

"We got to be careful how we act in front of him," Loris said.

Calvin drove the truck with the John Deere on it to Tobaccoton. The farm-implement agency was owned by Hap Turner, a big-bellied man who summers wore sport shirts, suspenders, and khaki pants. Hap shook everybody's hand. He'd have shaken hands with a power pole if it had one.

"Calvin, how's the missus?" Hap asked, sitting in his office. A crankshaft was propped against the desk, pistons were spread on the file cabinet, and a carburetor lay disassembled across his blotter. Hap was a soft man, his flesh fair and hanging, but behind the pale blueness of his eyes was no fat. "And that whip-arm boy of yours?"

Hot days Hap pulled a white handkerchief from his hip pocket, knotted the corners, and draped it over his head.

"Last I seen they was fine," Calvin said. He and Hap had done business since Calvin bought his first plowpoints and seed drill, so long ago it was beyond counting. They'd fished together, though Hap never tried to master the fly rod. He was a cane pole and worm man. Meat was what Hap wanted on the table, not sport.

"Cal, it's bad," Hap said. "A retaining bolt got loose in there and has tore up your gears. Looks like somebody whacked them with a grubbing hoe."

"How much?" Calvin asked. His throat had tightened, and his palms felt greasy.

"It's embarrassing, the price of parts is out of sight." Hap adjusted his glasses, leafed through his thick John Deere manual, and fingered figures on a calculator that made a whining noise like pain. "I hate to get out of bed in the mornings knowing what I got to charge. Your best way is to go with a rebuilt job. Save you 35 percent."

"How much?" Calvin asked a second time, and thought about casting a long, lazy line onto a quiet green pond so far from work and worry the only sound would be the soft kiss of a fly settling upon clean water.

"Knocking off the odd pennies it comes to—" More whining from the calculator. "—seven hundred and fifty-eight dollars."

Calvin sat very still. His eyes misted like he was underwater, a bass in shallows of a pond Hap had just thrown a night crawler on top of, to gulp down and get hooked on. Before answering he hocked to clear his throat.

"Reckon you could carry me a while?"

Hap had a way of changing shape when dollars floated around him. His flesh firmed up. The desk, the calculator, the parts manuals grew sharper and seemed to become extensions of him, like they grew from his body.

"Cal, I got to tell you stomachs around here has been rubbing backbones, and you're on my books now for a chunk of credit, the balance on your baler. You'd do better by both of us finding the money somewheres else. I tell you the truth, if I wasn't already in this business so deep I can't get out, I would. It's no fun anymore."

"Never been fun for me," Calvin said.

"I wish I had me a government job where all I had to do was show up mornings and go home nights. I tell you I don't like doing this to you."

"I don't like you doing it to me neither," Calvin said.

Hap walked him to the truck, shook his hand, and stood looking after him. Calvin spat and thought. He drove through Tobaccoton, past the spinning mill, the block of stores, and the stone courthouse with its bell tower. He parked behind the brick-and-glass Howell County Bank, again feeling his throat close, his palms ooze. He pictured waters no wind ruffled.

He knew banker Ed Amos from way back. They had bird hunted together, and when Ed's lawyer son ran for the state legislature, he came to Calvin for the family votes and got them.

"I don't even keep dogs now," Calvin said, thinking he could hardly afford to put meat on the table for him and Loris. He was again sitting in front of a desk. It seemed all his life he'd been sitting on the wrong side of desks, though this one was as dusted and orderly as Ed himself, a close-shaven, shiny man whose baldness made him appear even more polished up, like simonized metal.

"You read the papers and hear the radio," Ed said. "You got to be aware the banks around here are loaned out. Maybe if you didn't already have the note on your farm we could squeeze you a few more dollars, but till that's paid off, I think we'd be doing you a favor not to allow you to overextend yourself."

"Thanks for the big favor," Calvin said.

He drove back not to the farm but to his brother Claude's place seven miles down the road, in Bethel. Claude was a section foreman for the Norfolk Southern Railroad, heavier, though younger, than

Calvin, with an unhurried ease about him that rested on a steady paycheck.

"You asking me for money when Linda Sue and me just built a brick house and she wants to put braces on the twins?"

Calvin tried an uncle, a first cousin once removed, the banks in Clarksville and Chase City, other tractor dealers, and the Farm Credit Association. What'd happened to his reputation as a man who paid his bills? Toward the end he spoke the words automatically, knowing they weren't going to do any good but having to keep on because when he got home Loris would ask had he knocked on every door.

"I did and some," he told her in the kitchen, where she whittled corn from a roasting ear, quick, sure female slices of the knife that spilled kernels tapping into a pan, leaving the cob pale and bleeding its milk. He hated looking at his fields, which needed cultivating, and the low grounds that had thistles and broomstraw growing up because he couldn't pull his bushhog without a tractor. The land was already sour from needing lime. Where was he supposed to get lime from, stones?

He shivered in the heat at the thought of losing his farm. He pictured peaceful blue waters and a great silver fish slumbering under the surface. Sure it was a dream, but what did you do when sweat burned your skin raw and the damn weeds grew faster than you could chop them? Once he would've had a mule in the barn, but the tractor had slicked him into a trap. No farmer was able to make it any longer without machinery. Calvin might borrow equipment from neighbors, yet it was humiliating, like begging bread at the back door.

He hoed his garden. Jap beetles had stripped his snaps and were chewing his butterbeans. What did a man sow for, to feed bugs? He wanted to throw down his hoe and just sit, maybe a whole day, but Loris might be watching from the kitchen. She made him feel guilty about resting.

She made him feel guilty about fishing too. Even when he lugged home a bass big enough to feed them two meals, she acted like he'd been funning. She wasn't content unless he was breaking his back pinching off suckers, digging tatters, or pounding tin on the barn roof. He felt guilty about lying down at night and getting sleep for his weary body. He thought of Dip Cooley.

"You're not dealing with Dip!" Loris said, slapping her palms against the sheet. "I'll go to the mill."

"I won't have a wife of mine working at no mill!" Calvin said. They might as well nail a sign to the front fence announcing he wasn't man enough to provide for his family.

"Only till Wesley finishes college," Loris said, and next day drove the pickup to Tobaccoton to hire on. She worked second shift, from four in the afternoon till midnight, which meant nobody home to cook his meals or lie at his side. When he got up, she was still folded in the bed. What was he supposed to do while she saved money enough for the tractor, grub up kudzu and Johnson grass with his nose?

He knew Loris was thinking he could go to the mill hisself, but all his life he'd worked in the open air. He was no linthead. He'd die staying cooped up all day like a setting hen. Spinning was women's work. The men came out the mill hunched and ghostly. Their eyes didn't rise to another man's.

"The Lord helps those who help themselves," Preacher Sneed said from the pulpit, and glanced at the roof as if expecting the heavenly host to agree.

He sure helps some more than others, Calvin thought. He'd given up all he could—cigarettes, a beer or two Saturday nights, his hunting dogs. Loris was the only one bringing in cash money and hardly talked to him. He let Ben Buford go, Ben a runty, bowlegged black who helped around the farm and had lost two fingers from his left hand in a hammermill.

"Need me, just holler," Ben said as he slid into his old Chevy to drive off, and Calvin felt envy. Simple Ben was, but he didn't plant crops or study money. He was free to sit in shade of his pines. He could go fishing when he wanted. Lord help me, Calvin thought, I am so far down I am jealous of a poor, lopsided nigger.

Loris gave up her telephone, partly, Calvin believed, to shame him. He thought of himself walking through the mill gate and taking off his hat to enter the employment office. Once inside that sprawling gray building, he'd never come out. He'd be full of lint, tasting it day and night, and he'd smell like yarn and stinking dye.

There was nothing else. They had him holed. All right, for Wesley he'd do it. Calvin would try to hire on the same shift as Loris so they could save gasoline. She'd talk to him again, and he could assign his wages to Hap Turner for fixing the tractor. Calvin would be too tired to use it, but at least it would run.

He made his decision Friday afternoon as he mended a barbed-wire fence his bull had horned. While he rested, he watched buzzards circle in the pale sky and thought maybe they were keeping their mean, ugly eyes on him. He shouted, but they coasted on with their everlasting patience.

He heard a car and shaded his face to peer at it. Some car, a white Lincoln Continental with a whip antenna, fog lamps, and enough chrome to make a blind man see the light. Calvin crossed the barn lot towards it. The glass was tinted, the upholstery a blue velour, and the windows were rolled up to hold in coolness of the air conditioning.

A door at the driver's side opened, and out stepped another kind of buzzard—Dip Cooley, who wore a white suit with vest and a pearly western hat. He had on black cowboy boots squared off at the toes as if axed. Good thing Loris wasn't home. She wouldn't have allowed Dip on the place.

"Brother, if it gets any hotter we'll all catch fire and go up in smoke," Dip said, he tall and so thin you couldn't see much more than a line when he turned sideways. His face was a slab the color of ham fat, the eyes wet slate sunk back deep enough for shadows. Dip, a local boy, had left the county early because of trouble with a redhead girl in the rear of a school bus. After it was safe for him to visit his mother, he started coming back, always in big cars with different license plates—Georgia, Louisiana, Florida—and usually having a lady sitting beside him, the last one with hair piled bright as sawdust freshly fallen from the blade.

Dip reappeared on no schedule. He never told exactly what he did to put beans on his table, though he talked of land, oil, and dog races.

He picked his painted women, Loris claimed, to match his cars, just as he chose the trim or upholstery. Still, he took good care of his mother.

"I tell you it looks like ruin and desolation around the county," Dip said, using a long, thin thumb to push up his hat brim. "Makes me feel bad things has been going so good in my part of the world. Nothing but high hog. Catching you any fish?"

"If I was to meet one face to face, I wouldn't recognize a fish," Calvin said. They had sidled away from the cool, sweet-smelling Lincoln to the crackly grass in tattered shade of the red oak.

"Well shoot, Cal, I don't mean to mess in your business, but while I was gassing up down at Hap Turner's he mentioned you have a tractor needs fixing in his lot. I thought I been knowing old Cal a long time and maybe can give him a hand."

"You come to help me?"

"I hate seeing a fellow Howell Countian in a rough spot, surely I do."

"You don't have a woman in your car this time."

"No, Francine stopped in Lynchburg to visit her baby sister. I'm picking her up this afternoon for a drive to Baltimore to see about a boat. You know me, Cal. I always been obliging and hate worse than snakes seeing people in trouble. It purely tears up my insides."

"You offering to loan me money?"

"Better than money," Dip said, and reached into his vest pocket to draw out a black cigarillo, which he held to Calvin. Calvin wanted it but feared Loris might scent smoke on him. Dip's little finger bore a diamond stud ring, and a gold watch big as an egg yolk was strapped to his skinny wrist. From another pocket he slid a silver butane lighter that made a little hiss. He puffed, squinted at his fire, and hooked thumbs in his vest. "Cal, how'd you feel about having a new tractor standing out there in your shed, a top-of-the-line International diesel with both high and low ranges and eight forward speeds?"

"You come here to sell me a new tractor?"

"I'm here to trade one that's got less than a hundred hours on the engine, not a scratch on the paint. Nothing but good about it. Ladies see you on that tractor, they'll chase you up a tree."

"And you carry the payments?" Calvin asked, hope rising despite mistrust.

"That's the best part," Dip said and clamped the cigarillo in his speckled teeth so he could talk around it and not have to unhook his thumbs from his vest. "Won her in a little card game down Georgia way, a friendly contest with a bunch of boys working the tobacco market. Feller light on the pot asked if he could put in a chit for his tractor. Now what am I going to do with a tractor? I don't ride 'em anymore. Dirty up my pretty clothes. I'd have sold her before this except that feller forgot to send along his title. I'll catch up with him any day now and get it for sure."

"No title?" Calvin asked.

"Who cares about a little old piece of paper? You can use this tractor twenty years, drive her right into the ground and leave her rusting in a ditch. What's the difference if you're not selling or trading? Nobody's going to ask for the paper, and you'll get a thousand times your money's worth out of her around the farm."

"Suppose she's stolen?" Calvin asked.

"Now hold it a minute, don't go saying that. You don't know, and I don't. What's more I don't care 'cause I won that tractor fair and square in a game of five-card. Some things you don't have to put names to. You need a tractor, I got one that'll tickle you from toes to tonsils. If you don't want the favor I'm trying to do you, just say the word, but all I'm asking is your broken-down John Deere in trade."

"And my good title so you can have her repaired, make a legal sale, and pocket the cash."

"Cal, I won't be wasting anymore of your time," Dip said, and waggled the cigarillo between his teeth. He moved in thin, angular strides toward the Lincoln. "Remind me not to worry about you ever again."

Let him leave, Calvin thought, but as he stared out over his shriveled front pasture going to milkweed, and pictured tangles in the low ground, the tobacco that would need to be pulled and cured, and his ragged crop of sorghum, corn, and soybeans, he called after Dip.

"I got to see the tractor first!"

"You'll kiss me for her," Dip hollered back through the whirled-down tinted window. "She'll do everything except tie your shoes and love you in the bed."

Tuesday, while Loris was at work, the tractor arrived on a dusty lowboy with Arkansas tags and a Mexican driver. She was shiny as a new dollar. Calvin climbed onto the cushioned seat and drove her around the house. He tested all the gears, the hydraulic, the power takeoff. She was everything Dip promised, and it was more than Calvin could do to keep from laying his hand on her flank and stroking her like he would a fine horse. He had to have her.

"And I do believe in time I'll get you the title," Dip said. "I surely mean to work on it."

Calvin walked into his house and up the steps, lifted his title out of the shoe box in the bedroom closet where he and Loris stored important papers, and used the hot hood of Dip's Lincoln to sign over the John Deere.

"Cal, you my kind of people," Dip said, and his slate eyes flickered like electricity arcing gaps. For a second Calvin felt uncertain, even scared, but Dip was already folding the title into an inside pocket of his white suit, and there was that beautiful International gleaming like fresh blood in the sunshine. When Dip drove off, he waved and tooted. The Mexican in the semi followed out the lane, shooting dust as high as the cedar tops.

Now Calvin had to explain to Loris, and the next morning after he started the tractor, she hurried right out into the barnyard barefooted and wearing her drab cotton nightgown. Her dark, frizzy hair pointed ten different kinds of ways.

"Hap just turned you loose on a new one?" she asked. "All you had to do was trade in yours?"

"What matters is we come to an agreement," Calvin said, slipping her questions and busying himself with the hitch and bushhog so he wouldn't have to look into her green, drilling eyes. He felt bad, but she didn't have to know everything. He revved up and drove towards the low grounds, leaving swirls of blue diesel smoke and pretending he couldn't hear Loris over noise of the engine.

The tractor changed his luck. The same night they had a good soaking rain, the kind that falls slow and seeps deep to feed roots. Moisture revived his corn. His tobacco took on the heavy, brooding quality of good leaf. Then, lo and behold, late in the summer, crop prices firmed as the Japs bought beans and the Ruskies wheat.

He rolled his tractor among his rows, daring to believe he was going to make some real money, have a little jingle in his pockets after paying all his bills. Dollar signs bounced about in his brain like musical notes. He hired Ben Buford back to work around the place.

When in November Calvin sold his tobacco, he talked Loris into quitting her job at the mill. She was already being nicer to him. He began to catch whiffs of perfume, and opened the bathroom door to find her painting her toenails. Saturday night he drove her to Tobaccoton for a dance at the Moose Hall, bought them both a beer, and home shucked her out of a new pink satiny gown. He even roused a twitch and moan from her.

Wesley hitchhiked for Thanksgiving. He and Calvin drove to town and the barber shop. Calvin watched full of pride as the boy sat in the chair and politely answered men who came in off the street to question him. Wesley was already different from Calvin and Loris, with a kind of shine on him, like people who sat on the right side of desks. Calvin was so proud he felt stuffed.

"My slider's working fair, but I had to lay off the knuckler," Wesley told the men. "Last one I pitched got hit over the fence, the railroad tracks, and the water tank."

It was the best thing Calvin had, walking up and down the street beside his boy, stopping along the way to shake hands and chat. That's what life was about, a son you could respect and be respected by, an upstanding young man, no bragging, no flash, a boy straight and solid as white oak. Some things after all did work out.

When they drove home to the farm in the hot fall sunlight, Ben

Buford was using the tractor to pull the manure spreader up from the low grounds. Calvin and Wesley intended to fish, to get them a last bass or two before a cold snap sent the lunkers deep into the pond to wait out winter. Loris would be back soon from having her hair done, and start cooking up a storm. But Ben, flies spiraling around him and the spreader, cut the tractor engine. He had something to tell.

"Four of 'em," he said. "Drove right into the field to look at the tractor. Two was state troopers. Asked what happened to the ceral number. I told them the only ceral I knew about I ate for breakfast. They crawled underneath. Checked everything but the gas and oil."

Calvin stood very still. For a moment it seemed air, sound, the flight of birds had stopped. When life returned, sunlight appeared to drip as if melted, and his body filled with a hot sickness. His head became heavy, his neck stiff, and he felt the land under his feet had tilted. He had the crazy thought of stepping onto the tractor, driving it into the woods beyond the low grounds, and burying it so deep it couldn't be found and Wesley would never have to know.

Instead he drove his pickup back to town and climbed the jarring stone steps of the courthouse. Franklin Harper, the Commonwealth's Attorney, was in his office, a freckled young man whose red hair resembled fine steel wool with a wave in it. Calvin told him about the tractor.

"I didn't know it was stolen," Calvin said.

"Well, hell, let's admit you hoped it wasn't," Franklin said.

When Calvin drove home, he sat Loris and Wesley at the kitchen table and told them. He believed Loris would throw a fit, but she stared, rose to cross to her stove, and finished fixing supper. Wesley didn't say much. He looked past Calvin out the back door in the direction of the pines and pond.

"I honestly never knew for sure," Calvin said.

"You must've been pushed into it," Wesley said.

"Jail, will you have to go to jail?" Loris asked.

He did have to stand in the courtroom before peevish Judge Oliver and the town trash, who came in off the street to watch the free show. His throat choking, Calvin pleaded guilty. The judge sentenced him to three years' probation, fined him $2,500, and ordered forfeiture of the tractor.

"Calvin, you just ought to have known better," Judge Oliver said. Loris and Wesley stood beside Calvin in the courtroom. They walked out together.

He sold his crop, stock, and equipment to pay off the fine and his debts, and leased his land by going shares with neighbors so he and Loris could take jobs on the graveyard shift at the knitting mill. Loris never once mentioned Dip Cooley, who there was a warrant out for but couldn't be found. Sometimes Calvin caught her peering at him as if he was on the auction block and she wondering what price he'd bring. When rarely he went to town, men fell silent in the barber shop. He held his head up and looked them all in the eye, yet felt a drag at his face, a bend in his back, a weight like he carried a load.

During the spring Wesley signed on with the Peninsula Pirates. He was, he admitted, considering not returning to college. He explained he could do better playing ball. He didn't come home so much, though he did continue to write a postcard a week and tried to get them to accept money. In late August, Calvin and Loris drove the pickup west to Salem for a game. During the seventh inning Wesley hit a triple. Afterwards he took them out for a steak dinner to a fancy Roanoke restaurant that served liquor and had gold mirrors and ocean pictures with sailboats on the walls. It seemed to Calvin his and Wesley's eyes warped away from each other, as if they were looking around corners.

Back home, Calvin went fishing a few times alone. Loris didn't fuss. She might just as well have. Cast after cast of the whispering line he made to the arched, motionless willows, but found no pleasure in it. All the magic seemed to have fled his wrist. He stood his fly rod in a corner of the tool shed. Nights on the job, as he hurried among the humming, clicking rows of the mill's unforgiving white spindles, he hardly had time to think of the gathering dust.

altarpiece

Before Kate died, Peck experienced visions of himself standing alone on the wet, windy deck of their bay cottage. He would look to the bronze marsh and see flights of blackies and canvasbacks spiraling down from the cold, metallic dusk. He felt guilty about it. Certainly he never wanted her to die.

She did so easily as he sat by her bed in the private room of a Richmond hospital. Only moments before, they talked. She asked about snow, but no snow fell. She closed her eyes, Peck thought, to rest. As he read the newspaper, he heard her sigh, and when he raised his face, he saw her breathing had stopped. He ran for the nurse, but Kate was dead past all mortal doing.

After the funeral he gathered his son and daughter at the Cumberland farm to tell them he would have to sell it because he planned to live in the cottage beside the Chesapeake. That cottage, reared on pilings, was small, tight, and economical. They sat in the twilight parlor of the century-old house he and Kate had bought thirty years before, a two-story structure with no classic molding or wainscoting, yet solid as its hand-hewn white-oak joists and indestructible sun-kilned bricks made of clay from what was now the back pasture.

"Daddy, isn't there another answer?" Maggie asked, she twenty-eight, tanned and slim despite two children of her own. Tennis and fox hunting did that for her. She hadn't cried during the funeral, but later he heard her weeping in the second-story room where she lived her childhood, a place of curled snapshots, dried corsages, and a few last stuffed animals sprawled about.

"Rent the house and let somebody work the land?" Alex asked, he a trust officer with a Richmond bank. Alex was gaining weight, his skin agleam from the richness of corporate life. He wore his Washington and Lee tie. His hair, sandy like Kate's, was so obedient all he had to do was pat the strands to make them obey.

"I wouldn't want to rent," Peck said. "This farm needs people like your mother and me, who put ourselves into it. It requires family blood. Since neither of you can take it up, I see no alternative."

Peck found the right buyer in a young doctor and his wife who were moving to the county from northern Virginia. The energetic, jodhpur-clad wife wanted to raise Appaloosas, and the couple would have enough money to maintain, if not improve, the property. The sale was quickly closed. Peck gave as much furniture to Maggie and Alex as they could digest into their households. Kate's clothes went to Goodwill Industries. He contracted with a Lynchburg auctioneer to dispose of the remainder.

Peck didn't stay around that day in early April. He drove his car to Charlottesville and back to keep his mind from settling, to have something in hand, to fill his turbulent, collapsing center with the numbing hum of tires over pavement. Let it go, he told himself. Let it go.

When he returned to the farm that evening, the sale was finished. Everything had been sold, some pieces cheaply, most bringing more than expected. Paper cups lay about on the grass. He collected and burned them in the wire incinerator behind the house.

The morning he left for good, he didn't look back at his split-rail fences, the midnight green boxwoods of the garden, or the red hay barn. Still, the sorrow he'd been able to withstand reached out and caught his stomach like a claw. He guided the Oldsmobile to the side of the highway and cried into shaky hands. A pickup driven by a white-haired black man slowed and drew alongside. "You need help?" Peck, unable to speak, shook his head.

He drove on to the cedar cottage built at the tip of wooded land thrust into a harbor off the bay. Shiners thrashed, gulls whirled squabbling above sunlit water, and great blue herons waded like royalty in procession among glinting shallows of the greening marsh. He baited his crab pots and set them out. He wasn't yet strong enough to face memory because when he opened his mind even slightly, all the past with Kate, from the day they stood before the altar and swore the enduring oath to that last moment when she asked about the snow, came rushing at him like a wall breaking before a flood. Memory left him run over and bleeding.

His third Sunday at the bay he drove to a rural, steepled church that had daffodils and azaleas blooming around the doorway. The church sat in a meadow several miles south of Milford, the county seat. He tried to follow the sermon, which had to do with grace undeserved yet freely given, but it was too theologically complex and doctrinal. What he needed was balm, not reasoned argument. He kept hearing the words "Out of His infinite mercy and compassion." Again and again, "Out of His infinite mercy and compassion."

Leaving, Peck shook the minister's dry, lean hand and started for his car. A voice called. He didn't know the woman, who must have overheard him give his name to the preacher. She looked fifty, her hair curly red, her skin fair and freckled. Her shoes, dress, and hat were blue. Easter clothes, he guessed. She held her hands folded in front of her waist as if she had something captive in her palms.

"Jenny Coates," she said, and parted the hands to offer one to him. "We're so delighted you worshipped with us. We're having a picnic behind the fellowship hall. Won't you stay and break bread? You'll find no finer fried chicken in the state of Virginia."

He made excuses. He wanted no associations, not yet. The wrong word, a simple gesture, might bring down the wall. He backed away.

Tuesday morning, Jenny Coates came calling. Tires of her rusty beige station wagon crackled over oyster shells of his pine-shaded lane. She climbed steps toward his deck, her quick knees punching her yellow skirt. Her face was full and rouged, her hips broad and working mightily as she rose. There was a blowsy quality about her as if she'd passed through a high wind, though the air remained calm.

"We want you!" she said, smiling and pointing a finger at him. She puffed from her climb. "We have a loving congregation and are not about to be ignored. Plain honest folks—farmers, watermen, their ladies. Some families lived on this land before the American Revolution."

He didn't invite her in but stood on the salt-treated deck listening and effectively blocking her. Finally he said he had to drive to Richmond on business, not entirely a lie. Most of his income came from rents—he owned the best part of a commercial building—but he wasn't needed in the city more than twice a month.

He didn't return to the church. Jenny Coates telephoned to invite him to a crabcake fiesta, and he told her he would be out of town. During the early summer he saw her at the Milford Safeway. She had on a sleeveless orange blouse, a flowered wraparound skirt, and leather sandals. Her toenails were painted orange. Costume jewelry jangled and glittered.

She smiled as she lifted a can from a shelf to check the price. The smile was automatic, a face, he assumed, worn in her sleep. When she left, he watched through the store's poster-patched window while she transferred groceries from the cart to her station wagon. She wiped sweat from her neck.

That same week, as he repaired his dock, a worm-rotted plank broke under him, and he fell. He was able to drive to the emergency room of the Gloucester hospital, where an X ray showed no fracture but a severe sprain. While he waited on the examination table for a nurse to strap his ankle, Jenny Coates hurried in, talking even before he saw all of her.

"I heard at the launderette!" she said. "Why didn't you phone for help? Living alone is dangerous. Suppose you suffered a heart attack?"

She wore a lime shirt, white slacks, black heels, and more costume jewelry. She had apparently groomed herself for him, yet he was again struck by her blowsiness. She was a person in a perpetual fight to keep herself neat.

"You need someone to drive you home," she said, and lifted his right wrist to check his pulse as if herself a nurse. Her jade green eyes were never still.

He told her he could do it fine, thanks. She forced him to keep refusing.

"Give me their phone numbers, and I'll notify your children," she said.

"How do you know about my children?" he asked. Had she been snooping?

"We're small town," she said, not embarrassed but smiling. The smile wasn't convincing below those wild, roving jade eyes. "Can't hide anything from us."

She lifted a pad and pencil from her oversized canvas pocketbook. He insisted there was no need to upset Maggie and Alex. Jenny asked who would cook for him. Peck said he'd be able to get around all right. He felt crowded, as if she might crawl onto the examination table with him.

He rented crutches from the pharmacy and soon handled them well. Meals were no problem because he ate simply anyway: an egg for breakfast, a bit of meat in a sandwich at noon, and after his evening drinks a salad and two vitamin pills. Since Kate's loving fingers no longer touched his food, it was tasteless to him, merely fuel for the body.

Jenny made another visit to bring bread she had baked, the loaf in a red tin decorated with gaudily painted tulips. First she peered through the screen door, shielded her eyes, and called his name— not his last, his first name, Peck. Once she was in the cottage, he couldn't get her out of the kitchen till she had washed his dishes, pans, and pots.

When at last rid of her, he watched her drive away under pine shadows. Taillights wobbled, and she almost ran the station wagon into the ditch. He crutched back to the kitchen to unwrap and chew a bite of her bread. Though warm from the oven, the loaf was dry at the center. On his dock he crumbled the bread to cast on the water. Minnows seized it from below, and swift, raucous gulls banked down to snatch it skyward.

When his telephone rang that evening, it was Alex calling from Richmond.

"This woman rang me up," he said. "A Mrs. Coates. You need me?"

"I don't, and she's making too much of my situation." How had Jenny learned Alex' number?

Peck had hardly hung up before the phone rang again. As he hobbled to it, he knew it would be Maggie.

"Who is she, a neighbor?" Maggie asked.

"A force of nature she is, a nor'easter," he said, and they laughed.

He did need somebody to clean and hired a Mrs. Tessie Fitchette, wife of a waterman, to run the vacuum, wash clothes, and do windows streaked by salt spray. He still had Jenny's bread tin and worried how to return it without becoming trapped. Mrs. Fitchette was the answer. On her way home she could drop it off at Jenny's house in Milford.

Short and stout like most county natives, Mrs. Fitchette had a face like weathered driftwood. She seemed humorless, yet loved gossip.

"Better duck," she said while sweeping the deck around him as he sat sunning himself. She slid her cunning gray eyes at him and grinned, the change of expression hardly less startling than if she had removed her clothes.

From Mrs. Fitchette Peck learned Jenny had married three times and that her second husband, a French and Spanish teacher at the high school, had shot himself. The first husband was a dentist, the last, recently divorced by her, a Navy chief stationed at Norfolk. Jenny once won a beauty contest, her father had owned a boatyard, and there'd been money in the family.

"Spent every dime and dollar that came her way," Mrs. Fitchette said, as if extravagance were the one unforgivable sin. "Cars, clothes, putting on the dog. No woman's man was safe while she was on the loose."

Jenny now made her living peddling cosmetics door to door. Mrs. Fitchette twitched her broom and sniffed.

"Won't let you not buy nothing," she said. "Allow her in your house, she outsits you. Will not go home till you take out your pocketbook and pay her off. Not that she hasn't suffered, and people are part sorry for her, yet she still acts like she's beauty at the ball. Now she's on the loose again, you just better peek around corners."

Friday, when a vehicle approached the cottage, Peck did look from a bedroom window and recognized the rusting station wagon. He stepped backwards into shadows. Jenny rapped the brass knocker shaped like a canvasback's head, and called his name loudly. He feared she might enter and search him out.

The next Monday, driving to Richmond along a narrow county road flanked by ditches full of dark, mosquito-larvaed water, he spotted the station wagon half on the pavement, half off among weeds and purple-blooming thistles. Jenny stood at the front, hood up, and slapped at insects as she gazed perplexed into the engine well.

He was suspicious and would have driven past had not someone else been in the station wagon, a girl with long, ash-blond hair. Jenny waved both arms like a sailor on a sinking ship. He stopped ahead of the station wagon, backed to it, and got out. Though no longer using crutches, he still limped.

"I don't understand," Jenny said, her hands flapping. "We were driving to Gloucester, and this beast of an engine just died dead. My knowledge of automobiles is absolutely nill and void. I've never liked cars, and they don't like me. I believe they communicate in the dark, like cats sneaking around at night, conspiring to frustrate their owners. Oh, excuse my manners. I'd like you to meet my beautiful daughter Patricia."

Patricia sat as if alone in this world, her pale green eyes held level and staring ahead, a thin girl in her twenties, though it was difficult to be certain she wore so much makeup, especially around those eyes that appeared enlarged and threatening above her small, clenched mouth. Her shoulders were bare and bony. She seemed impatient, hard, furious.

"Can you tell Peck hello?" Jenny asked her.

"Sure, hello!" Patricia said, the words not spoken but flung.

Peck tried to start the station wagon. Jenny had already run down the battery. He had jumper cables in his trunk and knew engines, but wasn't about to dirty himself and miss an appointment in Richmond. "I'll stop at Port Haven and send help," he said.

"I so hoped it would be a tiny thing you could just tinker with and fix," Jenny said, her smile nearly failing, those jade eyes, much darker than her daughter's, widening to greater alarm.

"I don't give a damn!" the girl, Patricia, said suddenly. She wasn't looking at or apparently even talking to them but still stared straight ahead as if the object of her anger stood before her. "I mean I damn well don't!"

That was all. Chewing fitfully on her lower lip, the girl subsided into herself. Distressed, Jenny turned to Peck and lowered her voice as if in the presence of danger.

"We all have these days," she whispered. "You know, when nothing goes right. This morning there was no hot water and the milk soured."

He escaped quickly and stopped at the Port Haven Garage, where Jim Ligon, a dark, bearded man in gray coveralls, pounded a truck tire with an iron sledge.

"Who pays if I take the wrecker out there?" Jim asked, wiping his grimy hands on his thighs. "She's into me already for a bunch of money. Best thing she could do is push that heap into the ditch and walk away."

"You can't just leave them," Peck said. "Suppose I guarantee payment?"

"Up front. When she pays me, I give your money back."

Peck wrote a check for twenty-five dollars, laid it in Jim's hand, with its blackened fingernails that looked made from cattle horn, and asked that Jenny not be told. He then drove to Richmond for a conference with Hank Spaldin, his tax man. When Peck returned to the cottage that evening, his phone was ringing.

"So dear of you to send Jim," Jenny said. "How I detest automobiles! I'd like to drown them all. Some business about the gasoline filter being clogged. I promise to bake you another loaf of bread."

That night, watching a TV drama, Peck was seized with grief at sight of a wedding. The solemn words of the vow—''Whom God has joined together, let no man rend asunder''—brought the wall tumbling down, and he, awash in memory, stood on his deck and looked out over black, disturbed water to Wolf Shoal Light, whose gongs sounded like a death knell.

He grabbed his keys from the kitchen counter, hobbled down to his car, and drove the three hours to the farm. Back under ancient oaks a single light burned. He continued on to the cemetery behind the country church and knelt on grass over Kate's grave. He lay across it as if it were Kate's body. Somebody noticed his car and called the sheriff's department. A young deputy shone a spotlight on him, but then recognized Peck, apologized, and left.

At dawn Peck drove under a hot yellow sky toward the bay cottage. He felt emptied, gutted by grief. If he weren't holding to the steering wheel, he might drop away or float off, a husk to be blown by any wind.

He sought relief by working on plans for a new real-estate syndication. The figures were as insubstantial as smoke. He sailed his boat *Wayfarer*, named by Kate, into the bay and around Wolf Shoal Light. He found no pleasure in the Bristol's ease of handling, his own expertise, or the breaching of curving porpoises in hissing water beside the white hull. If tapped, his emptiness would resound like discarded tin.

When next he stopped at the Port Haven Garage, Jim Ligon strolled out to fill his tank.

''Hope you're not expecting your money back. She didn't even pay for the new filter. That daughter spends all the money.'' His expression became slyly lewd. ''Pat's laid half the men in the county. Maybe I ought to get in line and take out my bill in trade. Had a baby too not more than six months ago.''

Peck resolved not to stop at the Port Haven Garage again, and thought, so much trouble, so much misery for Jenny—those husbands, a wayward daughter, the frantic attempts to hold things together by selling cosmetics. He pictured her brave smile beneath those desperate jade eyes. Watch it, he told himself. In your condition don't go feeling sorry for her. Don't go feeling anything at all.

When she brought her bread, a Saturday morning in August, he was loading gear into the skiff to fish. Terns dove, splashed, and banked upward to the sun, their whiteness as shiny as porcelain. Mullet jumped from blueness of the sand-bound harbor. He hoped to catch the rising tide.

Jenny wore clean tennis shoes, tight Levi's, and a dark orange jersey with HOOS printed on it in black letters. Her red hair was frazzled. Bizarre she appeared, ridiculous, pathetic, yet the smile, always the smile, stayed in place, her shield.

"You're walking much better," she said. "Hardly a hitch in your step. Oh I love to fish. What's your bait? There's plenty of room in the skiff for two."

Her words rolled over each other with such speed it was difficult to tell where one sentence ended and another began. She made it impossible for him to refuse her coming along. She helped carry rods, bait bucket, and gasoline for the outboard.

Yet she knew the water. She cast off with a push from the dock, coiled the painter on the bow, and sat amidship to balance the skiff. Her flighty fingers became deft as she tied double clinch knots to rig her line and baited her hooks with minnows by fixing them through the lower lip so they would live and wiggle underwater.

She didn't look so grotesque out there in the hot light, the steamy, pungent marsh greenly gold behind her. Her excitement became boisterous when she hauled to the skiff a flounder weighing at least two pounds. She hooked an eel, which fell whipping to the boat bottom, causing her to lift her feet and shriek. He spied the girl in her, a momentary lifting of the veil, the phantom of youth in a vision of her dressed for the prom with an orchid pinned to the shoulder, or her wearing a satin-and-lace bridal gown in procession before the altar.

When they started back to the dock, she quieted. He didn't dare ask what bothered her. Perhaps land meant only trouble. She made the painter fast around a piling, unconsciously using a clove hitch, and turned away her face.

"My husband loved to fish," she said. Peck almost asked which husband. As she transferred gear from the skiff to the dock, he glimpsed her green eyes' wetness. She has known love, he thought, maybe more than I. All those husbands might have been dear to her. His anxiety about ridding himself of her was for nothing. She wrapped her fish in newspaper, repaired her smile, and left with a wave, the rattle of the station wagon dying among pines. A slight sunlit dust settled behind.

When a second week passed and he heard no word from her, his worry changed. Some new trouble in Jenny's chaotic life might have overwhelmed her. He would call to ask how she had enjoyed that flounder.

He had difficulty locating her. The number listed in the book, a recording informed him, was no longer in service. He tried the church, talked to the spare, brittle minister, a Mr. Gates, who told him Jenny had moved. He had no number but gave Peck directions.

"There have been reverses," Pastor Gates added. He volunteered nothing further.

The house was clapboard, hardly more than a box, near the boatyard. Its siding and tin roof wanted paint, the porch screen was torn, the grass needed mowing, and an outbuilding in the rear that had once been a garage or tool shed was being dragged down by honeysuckle and trumpet vine.

Embarrassment at seeing him flustered Jenny. Lemon-colored paint dotted her khakis. She'd tied a white cleaning cloth around her head. She threw up a cloud of words to hide the house's meanness.

"I love the out-of-doors!" she exclaimed, and lifted a palm as if presenting a paradise upon it. "I have garden privileges and next spring will plant English peas, tomatoes, and sweet peppers. I can live on salads, just crazy about them. Things need doing around here, but I enjoy the challenge of refurbishing. Smell that good air!"

He smelled turpentine on her and hot tar from the boatyard. The woman who owned the house, a Mrs. Palmer, was deaf and bent to a cane. Inside, a baby cried, whose Peck didn't ask, but he thought of Jenny's hard, painted daughter. Was she living here too?

On impulse he invited Jenny to dinner. Her hands, speckled with paint, flew about as if trying to escape being earthbound. She would be ready by six.

She kept him waiting on the porch that had the gashed screen and held only two straight wooden chairs. Down the dim hallway he spied the black, bulky sample cases she lugged about when selling cosmetics. Squawking fish crows flew over the house, grasshoppers pinged against screens, and at the boatyard a pile driver pounded with an absolute regularity felt through the ground.

They drove to Windy Point Marina, whose bluish restaurant windows looked out over a broad tidal river flowing smoothly to the bay. Sails flashed as boats drifted to moorings. She wanted red meat, not seafood. Being a native, maybe she'd become satiated eating fish. He remembered how she'd carried home that big flounder caught with him. Perhaps she was simply hungry.

"Your daughter living at the house?" he asked, again thinking of the crying baby.

"Patricia's left to take a government job in Washington," Jenny said.

She'd dismissed it too quickly and caused him to suspect he was being lied to, though the daughter could be gone anywhere, including to the dogs. Again he felt sorry for Jenny. An odd phrase formed in his mind as it occurred to him they shared great sadnesses: the fellowship of grief.

She, however, wasn't depressed, or at least allowed no wrinkle of dejection to settle on her active powdered face. While she chattered and reached for food, he nodded to encourage her. She told him how she loved flowers and once in a county pageant wore a gown made by pinning hundreds of red roses to a long, white silk slip. What I'm doing's better, he thought, than sitting home staring at the idiot tube. I know I'm alive, and we inflict no pain on each other—pangs of living that like the rain fall on the just and unjust alike.

They ate together now and again, nothing organized, usually at the marina, causing tight smiles among locals who knew Jenny. A quick, wet cold followed a warm autumn, and the first snow blew across chop of dark waters and patted the blue windows. Fishing boats grew ice on their stays and shrouds.

Christmas he visited his children and their families, but on New Year's Day he drove Jenny to the King's Arms at Williamsburg for a holiday feast. She was always perfumed and a bit overdressed. She had a weakness for enormous looped earrings. In no time he knew the range of her clothes and the inventiveness she called up to make her wardrobe appear extensive.

The desperate wildness of her jade eyes waned—a sign, he believed, of her gradual trust in him. He admired her optimism, surely forced as, hauling those heavy, misshapen cosmetic cases, she beat the bushes of the poor county for business. She never talked of her troubles. She was thinking, she said, of buying a new car, the beasts, and had ordered rose wallpaper for her bedroom. He wondered whether she had paid her bill at the Port Haven Garage.

Toward the end of January, when wind roughened the harbor with rolling whitecaps, and battered gulls took cover in lea of the marsh, Peck's son and daughter turned up at the cottage. They brought steaks, salad makings, and a bottle of wine. He built a fire of cedar and holly logs cut on the place. Alex donned foul-weather gear to hike out along the shore and gather oysters, which he shucked to be eaten cold on the half shell. Peck didn't realize they had come to check on him till his daughter led into it.

"So who's the girlfriend?" Maggie asked, her slim legs drawn up on the rattan love seat, a cup and saucer balanced on her suede thigh. "You do plan to introduce her to the family?"

"Spying on me?" Peck asked, both amused and irritated.

"No spies," Alex said, he too drinking coffee, the cup stilled beneath the sandy moustache he'd recently grown. "I do run into people at the bank. One mentioned you've been seen in the lady's presence. Dad, don't get miffed. In your present state of mind you can't be blamed. But do you know how many times she's been married?"

"My present state of mind," Peck said. "Would you enlarge on that?"

"It's been a year since Mom died," Maggie said. "We understand what that did to you."

"Her second husband shot himself, and the daughter's in a federal house of correction," Alex said. "Dope's involved."

"Okay, enough!" Peck said, standing. "I know what she is and I am. I also wonder whether my son and daughter are as concerned for their father's welfare as they are for their patrimony.''

He was being unfair. His children loved and respected him. They had a right to worry about the way he'd been acting. Gentling his voice, he assured them he wasn't about to lose his head. They stayed the night, and when they left early the next morning in a freezing rain, he hated seeing them go.

He recalled their words while having dinner with Jenny Saturday. Alex and Maggie could be correct about his state of mind, for Jenny looked pretty to him that night. She wore a ruffled white dress and, around her rebellious hair, a gauzy white scarf decorated with tiny golden stars. He had come to expect her to overdo it. Exaggeration in everything was her nature.

She had new earrings—silver trapezes with miniature bluebirds perched on them—and her costume jewelry jangled and reflected the restaurant's candlelight. He noticed the glow from her string of pearls against skin of her throat. He watched the curve of her fingers as they wrapped so femininely about the stem of her goblet.

She was full of talk. She had in mind opening a shop to sell locally made ceramics, wood carvings, embroidery. She'd been searching for rental space in Milford, but it was really only a question of finding a friendly banker. Should I, Peck wondered, provide the money?

She intended to make up catalogs and mail them out. He listened politely, yet as a businessman knew her plan wouldn't work. The county produced little in way of handicrafts, and there were too few tourists. She was spinning another dream, but the dream lighted her eyes, and she drank more than usual.

They drove through rain to the Gloucester movie, a sci-fi adventure into a dimension where disembodied spirits ruled a perfect planet. Returning home afterwards, she removed her head scarf, laughed at the absurdity of what they'd seen, and touched his arm as she talked. She must have freshened her perfume in the ladies' room, for her scent was strong. She leaned so near he felt her breath.

Her little house was veiled by a fine rain the wind warped across it. A light shone from a window feebly. The wind carried sounds of foghorns from the bay. He walked her onto the screened porch, which had yet to be repaired. Routinely he shook her hand, spoke his thanks, and waited for her to enter the door.

"Mrs. Palmer's visiting a granddaughter in Newport News," she said. "I'm sure she wouldn't object if you came in for a wee nip of John Barleycorn."

When he hesitated, she smiled, stepped to him, and raised fingers to his face. He thought it was to be a kiss on his cheek, but she turned his mouth to hers. The fullness of her kiss surprised him and caused him to jerk free. In opal light from the misted window, he saw her hurt and shame. She backed off from him, hands still lifted, bowed her head, and let herself in. As he called her name, the door closed and locked.

Her shadow skimmed away from the oval inset of glass. The house's darkness overlaid her. He left the porch, looked back, and opened his car door. On the seat lay a glaze, the gauzy white scarf. He brought it to the house.

When he knocked, she wouldn't answer. He tapped a car key against the glass. He draped the scarf over the knob. He stepped from the porch but instead of returning to his car walked through wet winter grass and blowing drizzle to the rear of the house and a faint light. As he held to the cold windowsill, he pulled to his toes.

Jenny lay on a single metal bed in a small room illuminated by a shaded seashell lamp atop a trunk. At the foot were paint cans with newspapers spread under them, her sample cases, an empty baby crib, and a roll of rose wallpaper. She'd thrown herself face down, and the hem of her dress bunched over the back of her knees. While he watched, the black pumps dropped from her feet one by one, each hitting the floor and overturning.

He'd never witnessed such sorrow, not even in himself—a pain that wrenched and shrank her body. She flinched as if being flogged. Her mouth's wail was soundless through the beaded window. Her suffering, he believed, came not from him alone. Rather, his rejection of her on the porch had been but the last step down a pitiless slope to a final, all-conquering despair.

He stood growing wet in piercing air that smelled of the boatyard and salt marsh. He walked to the porch and knocked gently at the door, then more loudly, finally causing the oval pane to rattle. The shrilling wind seemed to speak a refrain his own voice imposed upon it: "Whom grief has joined . . . Whom grief has joined . . . Whom grief has joined. . . ."

He banged till her shape approached the glass. She moved in her stockinged feet, a floating shadow, and opened the door a crack, at the same time attempting to hide her teary, frightened face behind fingers. He reached in to her, not with the hand holding the white, star-spangled scarf, but with the empty one, which closed strongly about warmth of her trembling forearm.

patriot

Each day no rain threatened, my father hung out his flag. If a storm later slanted through the shaded hollow, he would get word to us to bring the flag in, though that wasn't necessary because my mother, sister, and I knew to hurry to the front porch, twist the shellacked pole from a metal grasp screwed into the painted post, and carry the flag to our kitchen, where we rolled it around its staff and placed it in a dry, clean corner.

My father never served in the military. His had been a bugler during the Spanish-American War, and that solemn, devout soldier's face, topped by a floppy trooper's hat, sat ovally framed at the center of our mantel. My father had been too young for World War I, and throughout World War II he, a coal miner, was deferred by his draft board, yet pawed the ground to go. My mother and bosses at the mine attempted to argue him out of it, and when they couldn't stop him from volunteering, they secretly spoke to authorities in Jessup, who intercepted his papers and informed him he was too valuable to do without.

"You're serving your country," Mr. Jenkins Dabney, owner of the Mingo Collieries, told him. "The United States can't make guns, planes, and shells unless good men like you dig the coal."

So my father again climbed to the mine, sped into darkness, and that same spring bought his first flag, just a small one for our board-and-batten house perched middle way up the slope of a West Virginia

144

hill. It was a single-story, four-room Jenny Lind with a porch leveled by stones, the whole hanging onto that hill like a cracker box blown over the ridge and caught on a beech flat.

Forty-five wooden steps and a railing led down from the house into the dusty hollow, with its shiny railroad tracks and miners' dwellings along the shallow, meandering creek. Friends looked up to see sunshine on that flag and smiled thinking about my father. Later they thought something else. Often I woke blinking into rosy, misted rays of dawn and pictured my father moving like a phantom through haulways of the mountain's absolute darkness.

Yet he loved mining and never considered himself unfortunate. He wouldn't have understood had you sympathized with him for being exploited. The temperature in underground rooms was constant, winter or summer, and bosses left him alone instead of crawling over his back. In those days our men were still paid by tons shot down and loaded, not by the hour, and brass disks from the giant safety pin on his belt mounted at the weigh station like poker chips of a winning hand. It was manly work he could do in his own time and fashion.

He never mentioned black lung, roof falls, or firedamp. Men died, that's all you could say about life, he believed: men died. I doubt he thought about it much, though danger was ever present, a deadly spice to the day that workers in offices never know. The threat had to bring a special feel and smell to each shift survived as he walked from the mine darkness into the embracing, tree-scented air, and lifted his chunky minstrel face to the exploding brilliance of the lowering sun and to swift, tumbling clouds which made the mountain seem to be toppling.

Or when he and other men stood talking and joking under steamy showers of the company bathhouse, danger defied had to be part of a silent chorus, a canticle heard only in the mind. Arriving home, he always kissed my mother, his body still bearing odors of coal, strong soap, and an essence of cheating the mountain and death.

She didn't like his taking me to the mine. She wasn't ashamed of his work or more afraid for me than any other mother, but she

believed it time one man in the family did something else if he
wanted, at least have the chance.

"He's good with figures," she said of me. She worked in the high-
school cafeteria at Big Coal, my father claimed, just so she could cast
an eye on me and see I did right. "There's chance of a scholarship."

"You want him to go out and count money for a living like a
banker?" my father asked, kidding her. In his undershirt he sat on
the porch, hair dark along his muscled arms, a cigarette drooped from
his mouth, his shoes fallen to the floor. He looked over rain-washed
sycamores and willows to the creek and rails glinting in the cooled
hollow. "Why, he'll have to wear his vest to bed nights."

"Somebody ought to escape these mountains," she said. "He
might see the sun from its coming up to its going down."

They were married late. She was thin and wiry, her mouth snap-
pish, her hair chestnut brown, her eyes dark. Flapping her apron, she
had once driven off a bear feeding on thorn apples behind the house.
She didn't often become angry, but when so, everybody lit out for the
woods, including my father.

"Mad she makes dynamite seem puny," he'd say.

Yet she was pretty in a kind of dainty, even refined way. During
vacations, when my father drove us in his Ford to Virginia Beach to
stay a week in a three-story white wooden hotel, she really dressed up
and looked nice as any woman there, though more restrained of
speech, stiffer, faster of eye, as if expecting that bear to be behind
every stranger.

My father promenaded her along the boardwalk and, cigar in
mouth, sat himself to talk with other men on the long veranda's
wicker chairs, arranged among potted palms and polished brass
cuspidors. No fancy waiters or snooty guests intimidated him despite
his Mingo Mercantile clothes' lack of fashion, the large-pored coarse-
ness of his skin, and the raw, scarred roughness of his stumpy fingers.
His torso was short and thick, but he had a dignity, a refusal to back
off or bow that was like rudimentary nobility—perhaps, as my sister
and I preferred to believe, wild, fugitive genes that harkened back to
Highland chiefs or Irish kings.

Neither he nor my mother ever went into the ocean past their ankles. They stood at the water's edge and gazed at waves and surf, but to stick their white, towel-draped bodies into the foaming wash was to them unthinkable.

"Salt water toughens the skin," my mother said, she already honed by mountain winds to the hardiness of wild lilies of the valley that grew annually from rocky soil beside shaded, icy streams and falls.

"God knew what He was doing when He created fishes to do the swimming in the sea," my father added.

My sister Bess and I talked on the porch at home about what we'd become and do. She intended to be a nurse and take her training at St. Luke's in Bluefield. I wanted a business career that would allow me to live in a city like Beckley, Charleston, or Huntington.

"But we'll always come back," she said, a large girl, heavy of bone like my father, yet with my mother's chestnut brown hair and skin as clean as new corn.

There had been strikes before. Jessup County was union country, and for many mining men and their families spade-jawed John L. Lewis expanded the trilogy of God, Jesus, and the Holy Ghost. They pictured that thunderous, majestic face when they tried to imagine what the Lord looks like.

My father too was union but not crazy for it. He got along with Mr. Jenkins Dabney, mine owner and gentleman who lived in a stone house behind a wall on the mountain. My father argued against it when during World War II the United Mine Workers went out while Americans were still fighting in Europe and the Pacific. Men called him scab and broke his windshield, and goons jumped from laurel one night to beat him with pick handles. He staggered home bloody, his face bleeding, misshapen, and smudged from rolling in cinders, but his mind was unchanged.

"We're already getting paid ten times what the soldier boys are," he said. "If we got to strike, let's least wait till we win the war."

"But nobody'll give a damn about us then," Sam Waters, friend and officer at the local, said. "We got to get while the getting's good."

By train Franklin D. Roosevelt sent troops to operate the mines. That was when John L. said you couldn't dig coal with bayonets. He stood up to the entire U.S. government and won. Miners were drinking, hollering, and shooting off guns down in the hollow to celebrate, but my father bought another flag, a bigger one, and hung it on the porch for everybody to see.

His doing so was resented. My father could have been an officer in the union, he was that well thought of before the strike, but afterwards many people remembered how he had shamed them. The larger flag was a daily reminder.

Native hatred of owners and bosses did not live in my father. He was one of those special men who love physical work, the more difficult the better. He went at it not reluctantly but as if challenged. Pay to him was nearly an afterthought. Being best at what he took in hand fired his engine. No man loaded more coal or shot it down as cleanly. It was said he could use blasting powder so precisely he would have been able to blow his nose with it and never need to carry a handkerchief.

He whipped men and muscle but not technology. Revised contracts permitted installation of labor-saving equipment. Instead of coal being shot down and hand loaded, the new Joy and Jeffery machines chewed it out with iron-spiked teeth while duckbilled loaders scooped up a ton at a time and dumped it onto speeding conveyor belts for unassisted trips to the preparation plant. No longer did you see more than a man or two around the tipple, and where at shift changes cars and pickups traveling to and from the mine had raised a reddish dust, the air was now only hazy and the creek at the crossing barely muddied.

My father got reclassified as an electrician. He brought home fingered brown manuals with smeared pages to study, which my mother helped him with. He read slowly, laboriously, taking in words one by one as if lifting stones. At the kitchen table they puzzled over wiring diagrams. The yellow wooden pencil in my father's lumpy fingers seemed as flimsy and out of place as a china teacup.

"My brain's not used to this kind of work," he said, but it was more than that. He got along poorly with Milt Pritchett, a fellow electrician. Milt was younger, better educated, and impatient with my father's steady, deliberate ways. Milt didn't understand being gentle with a mountain. He never paused to listen to it talk. He attacked coal as if it were the enemy.

When a master coil burned out because a switch was thrown wrongly, he in a fit cursed my father. Now my father was about average coal-camp religious, but he didn't cuss much, particularly he didn't other people. There underground in the quick white sheen of his lamp, he stepped to Milt, grabbed him one-handed by the jacket, and slapped him so hard Milt's helmet was knocked off and his feet did a little sideways dance. "Milt," my father said, "you talk to me like that again and I'll prize open your mouth, reach down your throat to where your tongue's rooted, and rip her out for catfish bait. Got me?"

Milt had him all right. He never again raised his voice to my father and curved around him when they met. And he didn't forget either. Other men had seen his shame. My father made him realize his own meanness. So Milt kept complaining my father was slow learning the job and dangerous to himself and the entire shift.

When after the Korean War coal went bust, my father was one of the first let go. He tried to claim seniority rights, but those had got mixed up with changes in job classifications. The union could've helped. Trouble was he no longer had friends at the local, not after the second flag.

Then too during the fifties so many men weren't working in West Virginia that they became the Okies of the decade, bailing out of the state in rattletrap Fords and Chevys with mattresses and chairs lashed on top, the outflow just like from Oklahoma in the thirties except not to California but to the alien industrial cities of Pittsburgh, Detroit, Cleveland. Empty homes sat forlorn along the creek. My father, stubborn to the end, refused to leave.

"I'm not walking off from my house, garden, and chickens," he said. He and my mother raised only a few white leghorns, and their garden was a small plot dug flat into the side of the hill, not much more than 20′ × 20′, but still it provided a surprising amount of food for our table, no fatback-flavored snaps tangier, no roasting ears sweeter.

In the early sixties I was to enter West Virginia University at Morgantown. The family hiked out for a picnic at Hawks' Gorge, a deep cut in the mountain worn away over centuries by a dark, rapid river breaking white over boulders older than time. Steep the sides were, and the single set of railroad tracks appeared temporary, even fragile. Only a few trees were able to grow from cracks in rocks, those trees stunted, skinny, wind-deformed.

Every summer since I was a boy, my father and I had climbed down to the river and back, not a declared race, yet one that took some twenty minutes in the descent and more than an hour to the top. He always arrived first and hollered to ask had I broken a leg or what I was going so slow. I wasn't going slow. I clutched at rocks and tried not to think of the space like a hungry mouth below me.

He loved Hawks' Gorge, misty and bluish to the south, the trees on distant ridges gleaming with sun and moisture, the mountains a wilderness and sea of dark combers. The gorge drew a kind of poetry from him. "My ocean," he called it. "One I can swim in."

My mother spread a tablecloth on a broad, flat rock above the gorge and set out plates and cups as she prepared to serve the ritual meal for a son leaving to the big world. My father kept kidding me.

"So we got us a college boy," he said, poking my sister. "He already thinks he's smarter than the rest of us poor dumb hillbillies, yet I bet I can still whip him on a climb down to the river."

"I admit you're the champ," I said, and smiled at my sister.

"Proves you're smart there anyhow," my father said. "Now I confess I don't pray as much as I ought—"

"Amen to that!" my mother said as she spooned out fried apples topped with a glaze of brown sugar.

"—but I'm asking the Lord to look after our boy as He has looked after me in this life. I'll also ask him to keep tending to this blessed country, which in spite of the troubles we are passing through is the only place I know a man can walk around breathing free air twenty-four hours a day. Now if your mother don't hurry and pass me a drumstick I'm going to start gnawing on somebody's arm."

To my astonishment, bad times or not they had saved a little money for me. I received a partial scholarship from the university and worked afternoons in a drugstore, both clerking at the counter and helping in back with the books. Each Tuesday as regular as sunup a letter arrived from my mother, written prettily in blue ink on pale pink paper that had red rosebuds printed in the upper-left corner. I knew where she bought the paper. Year after year I'd seen it, wrapped in dusty cellophane, for sale at the Mingo Mercantile.

> We are all right. I still have my job with the school, and your father was lucky to find work doing construction on the turnpike. Bess, the chickens, and the garden is fine. Don't forget your prayers and go to church. Your father says don't get so smart it busts your head.

When I went home by bus for Christmas, the flag flew up at the house, and my mother was anxious because my father was thinking of mining coal on his own.

"Just a two-man operation," he explained. "I found me a good seam over Turkey Hollow way, and Pete Knackers, who owns the rights, will let me dig it on a royalty basis. I tell you, son, I not been the happiest man in the world since I left the mines. I need the smell of coal in my nose."

He and Robbie MacWhorter opened the side of the mountain. They hammered together a crude loading chute down the slope and slid diggings banging and spiraling black dust onto the dented bed of an old White dump truck bought to haul loads to the tipple. There was no bathhouse, and when my father returned home nights he was like a black man peering out of darkness, but he was happy. He again had his hands on coal.

The price came back some, and for a while he made money enough to pay off the truck and equipment—the little he had, for he still, like in the old days, shot down his coal with blasting powder, and he and Robbie used shovels to fill the rusty, bashed-in mule cars they pushed out on wobbly rails they'd laid.

When prices softened, both the union and companies pressured the tipples not to accept independent coal. They had to give in or black smoke would have risen everywhere. My father and Robbie drove the White all the way to Kentucky, where they could sell undisputed. At the same time government men landed on them about safety violations.

"That roof's not coming down," my father argued. "I put up those props myself, good locust posts cut right here on the mountain. Drainage'll never rot them. Fellows, they'll outlast you."

"Lack of ventilation and brattices," the inspectors said, young men making notes on metal clipboards.

"We not deep enough in the mountain to need fans yet," my father said. "Hardly out the sun, and you couldn't light your pipe with the gas in this mine."

But the inspectors cited him, and my father had to hire a Bluefield lawyer to fight it. The lawyer won because my father's mine was small enough to escape most regulations, yet there was time lost and legal bills, and when it came to the latter, no lawyer ever went broke. My mother wrote the check while my father paced outside and threw rocks down the mountain into the hollow.

My senior year in college he closed the mine. The old White gave up the ghost, and he could raise no money for another truck. Plus bowlegged Robbie got to drinking and crushed a foot by dropping a roof jack on it. Finally it turned out they weren't properly deducting Social Security, Withholding, Unemployment, and Workmen's Compensation, so the government claimed, and my father again had to go to the lawyers.

"Son, you in the wrong business," he said. I'd just hired on with Union Carbide in Charleston and rented a riverfront efficiency apartment. "Why, being a lawyer's like having a spigot connected to the money factory."

"You want me to become a lawyer?" I asked.

"God, no! I'll not wish damnation on any man, 'specially my own son."

He was still straight in the back and plenty strong, yet more deliberate in his moves. Coal prices spun upward in the industrial whirl of the Kennedy years, but my father had lost all rights at the union and besides couldn't operate the complex new equipment— great, grinding monsters that cost tens of thousands and gobbled up mountains like gigantic hogs rooting. Some men hired to run those machines had even attended college.

In past days my father might have appealed to Mr. Jenkins Dabney, but the old gentleman had died, his collieries sold by his children to an Ohio corporation that in turn was purchased by a Connecticut conglomerate. Mr. Dabney's house behind the wall was now empty and vine clasped. Sparrows and squirrels frolicked in great rooms once agleam with antiques and polished silver.

My father found work at the Highway Department. I passed him as I drove home in the first car I ever owned, a Plymouth coupe purchased by my posting payrolls for Union Carbide. I was courting a girl I expected to marry, a prim brunette named Dottie, the daughter of a Kanawha County assessor.

My father struggled to clear a drainage ditch beyond a cindered shoulder. Four or five men, all younger, stood about while he hacked away with a brush ax at briars and thistles in the ditch. Down his tanned face sweat flowed into strings, like glistening twine. Hating to get my new car dusty, I parked carefully at the side of the road.

He wouldn't come out of that ditch to chat. He waved, called my name, yet went on working. The other men were just leaning on their shovels and grubbing hoes, shifting their chaws as they watched and waited, and they smiled at me as if they didn't know what to do with him, as if he were a wild-spirited boy they couldn't control.

The next November the Republicans got voted into state offices, and out went the appointed Democrats in the Highway Department and those they'd hired to work on the roads. My father wasn't political except he believed Franklin D. Roosevelt was the greatest man who ever trod this earth, and kept a framed color magazine picture of him on our parlor wall. "He saved the banks," my father said, who never had much in any bank. "And he sent Hitler and the Japs howling. With him this country knew how to win wars."

Political or not, my father had always backed the Democrats because, he said, voting was like taking your pants off and on. Once you
had the habit of doing it a certain way, changing was hard.

He was again out of work. This time he didn't even try the mines
but found a job sorting lumber in the new furniture factory at
Coalton, which meant he had to drive thirty-seven miles over a road
so winding a rattlesnake would've had trouble making the curves. He
left before sunup and came home in the dark but joked about the
work. "After the mines it's like play," he said. "Why, it's so easy I
feel guilty about taking they money."

Then more union trouble, the curse of West Virginia. The factory
wasn't organized, but the employees were natives brought up in the
feuding UMW tradition of rule or ruin. They struck, smashed windows, slashed tires. After six weeks of violence, the factory closed and
hauled its machinery to North Carolina. My father was again looking
for a job.

He was nearing sixty, and the chance of anybody taking him on
was slight. Still he made the rounds, knocking on every door he could
lift a knuckle to. He tried to keep busy by painting the house, pointing up the chimney, and repairing the forty-five steps, many of which
had dry rotted.

I'd driven Dottie down to meet the family. She was tall, quiet, and
a little fearful of a mining hollow. Graduated with a degree in ele-
mentary education, she taught second grade in the Kanawha County
school system. My father made over her, opening doors and holding
chairs, and my mother wrung the neck of another white leghorn for a
picnic at the gorge.

Dottie was afraid to step close to the edge. She held her breath and
flattened a hand on her breasts to peek over and see the dark river
smash against the ancient boulders. She couldn't believe my father
and I used to climb down and back up.

"Why, we'll do it right now and show you," my father said.

"No you won't!" my mother said. "Not in those clothes!"

"Anyway I'm out of practice," I said.

"Here I'm giving him a chance to show off for his girl, and he won't take it," my father said, and poked Dottie. "Knows I'll beat him back to the top."

Later at the house he and I sat on the porch while the women cleaned up and talked in the kitchen. The flag, frayed and thin as gauze, lifted slightly, the sometime breeze southwest along the shadowed hollow. My father always listened to the evening news on his little radio. He was disturbed about Vietnam and resented being too old to serve.

"I won't have to go," I explained. "Luckily I have a high number, and then by September Dottie and I'll be married."

"You don't want to go?" he asked, his frazzled eyebrows lifting.

"It's none of our business. It's their war and stupid for us to get ourselves killed."

"That what you went to college to learn?"

"I learned some things in college, yes, sir."

"Like letting other men haul your coal for you?"

His voice caused my mother and Dottie to peep out from the kitchen, yet he stared at me not with anger or rebuke kindling his greenish eyes but in wonder—as if for the first time he realized I was more than just an extension of himself, of his thoughts and beliefs. We never again talked about it. Rather, he listened daily to his radio like a man facing wind. He also bought himself another flag, the third one. It flew bright on the hillside as a new patch on old cloth.

He attempted more free enterprise, this time whittling faces from chunks of stove wood picked from the pile behind the house. He owned an outsized book with a sun-bleached blue cover given him by his father, the bugler in the Spanish-American War. It contained drawings and pictures of all the presidents up through Coolidge. He sat on the porch, a rock weighing open the book to George Washington, and squinted in concentration as he worked away with a pocketknife, gouge, and plane. The face did resemble Washington, his nose lopsided, his white-ash periwig askew, if you had a hint ahead of time who it was supposed to look like.

He got my mother to bring a book from the school with the presidents from Hoover to Johnson, and during the winter labored long and hard to finish the entire thirty-six—dwarfish, ill-proportioned figures as grim as sin, except for Franklin D. Roosevelt, who had a jaunty cigarette holder and a smile cut into his face. Wood shavings were everywhere, and my mother followed my father about with a broom.

In the spring my father drove to the highway between Beckley and Bluefield to sell the carvings off the tailgate of his rattling Chevy pickup. Trouble was the turnpike had drawn about all the tourist traffic from that road, and though a few locals stopped to look, they didn't buy.

"Maybe I ought to paint 'em," my father said to my mother. He bought jars of red, white, and blue paint as well as a dip of pink for the glowing tip of FDR's cigarette. He dabbed at the squat, militant figures with a child's brush bought at the Mingo Mercantile.

"I don't expect a person to buy the whole set," he said. "But when somebody takes one or two, I can hurry to whittle out replacements."

Even painted the figures didn't sell, so my father drove up onto the turnpike itself, paid the toll, and parked in the concrete lot at the side of the Treetop House, an alpine structure of redwood and tinted glass where travelers bought gas, food, and novelties. He hoped to persuade the manager to sell the presidents in the gift shop. The manager, a dark slim youth who spoke a fast, different kind of English, said he didn't have the authority to display the items because Treetop House wasn't owned locally but by a company in Pennsylvania.

My father walked out to the parking lot to peddle the presidents off his pickup. That drew a crowd, and an elderly man from Tennessee offered him fifteen dollars for Franklin D. Roosevelt. My father talked him up to twenty-five.

As my father fitted the money into his wallet, the sheriff and a deputy arrived, red and yellow lights flashing. Somebody had complained, maybe the manager of the Treetop House, and the sheriff, balding and gentle, explained to my father he couldn't sell anything anywhere in the county without a merchant's license and that even with a license he wasn't allowed to set up shop on leased property.

My father drove to Jessup and paid the twenty-five dollars from

FDR for a license. He came back to the turnpike, forked over his toll a second time, and pulled into a scenic overlook above the Bluestone River. Again he set out the gnome figures of the presidents in formation on his tailgate. This time the state police arrived, also with lights flashing.

"The turnpike's an indirect instrumentality of the state," the trooper, an erect, heavyset sergeant, said. He wore dark glasses and glittered with the threatening paraphernalia of law enforcement.

"What about me?" my father asked. "I ought to be the instrument of something or other since I been paying taxes all my life. Looks like the state would allow me a few inches of ground."

"You can't set up a stand at roadside. Constitutes a traffic hazard."

"I'm a hundred feet from the road and didn't anybody ever tell you this is supposed to be a free country?"

My father had to carry his carvings back to the house. He pounded a sign into moist ground at the foot of the wooden steps: PRESIDENTS FOR SALE. Nobody climbed those forty-five steps to look except a few neighbors who'd already seen and didn't have money to buy. My father arranged the presidents on the mantel behind the picture of his warrior father, lined them up in three ranks, a stern platoon ready to march off against America's enemies.

He found work now and then, like being a poll watcher on election day or using a chain saw for Appalachian Power to clear a right-of-way straight as a knife slash through the wooded mountains. Some of his friends were on welfare, but even between jobs he wouldn't apply.

"I don't blame nobody, but I can't take money for doing nothing," he said. "Long as Mom and I got a garden and my shooting eye's good, we'll have food on our table."

Plus during the school year my mother brought home tote from the cafeteria. He didn't like that but ate silently. He stayed in the woods more. He'd already dug a root cellar and used scrap lumber from the old Dabney place to knock together a smokehouse. He meant to cure up enough venison hams to get them through tight times.

When he became eligible for Social Security and a tiny union pension, he and my mother were so frugal it was like finding riches. Still, he couldn't become used to being idle, to having no coal to take in hand, no tools to grip in his fingers. He painted each thing that could be painted, fixed all that could be fixed, and hammered every nail that could be hammered. He sat on the porch listening to the radio or in the parlor watching the TV my sister and I had bought him. He gloomed about Vietnam but kept the flag flying.

That February a freakish day dawned—sunny, still, warm. Ground thawed to slipperiness, and my mother half expected wild-flowers to spring from the mountainside. Then a breeze drifted up from the south, soughing past the leafless locusts and among shiny conifers. Mom said it smelled like the seashore, like Virginia Beach, and maybe the breeze had carried the ocean that far.

My father, stretching from a nap, took his Winchester from the closet but didn't come home that evening. My mother roused men to go looking. Just as quickly as the warmth came, the cold returned, icy grits of snow blowing in from the north, the wind shrilling over bare limbs and causing hemlocks to bend and groan. In the drifting skim of snow they couldn't track him till morning. First they found his Winchester leaned to a rock at the top of the gorge. He lay below among white boulders at the edge of the dark river. They didn't think he was bleeding because his body, turned on its side as if resting and serene, covered his own blood.

He might have been trailing deer, though no men hunted at Hawks' Gorge. There was no way to carry the meat up the side of the mountain. They brought my father out on a handcar loaned by the C&O Railroad.

My sister Bess wept and wilted beside me as we stood in the dusky, carpeted parlor of the Big Coal Funeral Home. She resembled my father much more than I, with her strong, stout body and a will that burned in her like a light. Her dress was stylishly black. She had a good job at a Roanoke surgeon's office.

"It's what they're whispering," she said. "Because his rifle was left at the top. Wouldn't it have fallen too?"

"Not him," I said, holding her and feeling the strength under her softness. "He never quit anything in his life."

"He felt so useless and was depressed about the war. Mom said that he worried more than he showed, that lots of times out in the woods he wasn't hunting at all but just sitting and brooding."

"He didn't jump," I said, squeezing her and seeing the fair down on her neck, cheek, and temple. "It was like a spring day, and maybe he was just climbing, remembering the good, having himself one last scamper up and down. He always thought he could do anything. He must not have realized how slick the rocks were. I know he didn't jump. If I know anything in this world, it's that."

The funeral was at the Mount Olive Baptist Church, near the head of the hollow. Hands clasped before them, a few mourners, mostly old people, filed past the casket for the view. My father's expression reminded me of the presidents on the mantel—firm, determined, brave. My mother stood straight as a sentry, but just before they closed the casket lid she wheeled, alarmed.

"The flag," she whispered when I lowered my ear to her.

"There isn't time," I whispered back.

"He would want his flag," she said.

They delayed the funeral while I drove fast to the house and ran up the forty-five steps. The flag wasn't flying, had been taken down and replaced by a black wreath. When out of breath I returned to the church, my mother laid the flag in the casket with him, not rolled but unwound so it spread over his chest and arms. She arranged it tenderly under his upthrust chin as if tucking in a napkin.

She didn't break till late that night when everyone besides Bess, Dottie, and me had gone. We heard her moving about, and peeked through the door to see her swaying, her fingers hushing the keening of her mouth. She stood staring at the mantel, where the dwarfish figures of all those presidents gazed out at attention, each gleaming a red-white-and-blue gloss in light from the single overhead bulb—except for a gap in ranks caused by Franklin D. Roosevelt, whom my father had never replaced.

the question of rain

The request came from an unexpected source during the dusty, choking summer. Wayland was in the backyard of the white frame manse. His wife, Mims, called through the kitchen screen door that Alex Bradner was on his way out. Oh damn, Wayland thought, because he believed he had at last educated his congregation not to bother him on Mondays except for illness or death.

Alex Bradner owned knitting mills, cinder-block plants that manufactured textured polyesters and spun down a fine, almost invisible lint over the flat Virginia town. When the mills worked three shifts, a person could look out at the early morning grass and believe it was frosted even in July.

"We might have to close unless it rains," Alex said to Wayland.

Alex was a hard-driving man in his mid-fifties, his impatience held in check only by his breeding. Even sitting in a lawn chair, Alex seemed in motion, about to leap up to do a job, to wrench the world to the shape his hands desired.

"I didn't know you used that much water," Wayland said.

"It's the dye," Alex explained. "We need water for our dyeing process, and if the river runs low, the discharge concentration is increased to where the Water Control Board in Richmond can shut us down. I'd like you to pray for rain."

Wayland almost smiled because Alex Bradner had little spiritual depth. He was generous with his pocketbook but not himself. During

160

services, rather than sing the hymns, he studied them as if they were corporate reports. He never recited the Apostles' Creed.

"Well, of course, I'll be happy to pray," Wayland said, the smile twitching at his lips. "Would you like to right now, you and I together?"

"I think it ought to be in the church," Alex said. His blue eyes seemed lidless they were so unblinking.

"All right, we'll walk over," Wayland said, prepared to stand. "Though I don't think it's necessary. I'm certain our prayers can be heard just as well from a backyard."

"I don't mean just us," Alex said. "I think you ought to make this Sunday a Special Prayer Day for Rain."

Wayland looked at Alex to see how serious he was. Alex wasn't frowning, but his face perpetually verged upon it.

"I don't think I'd care to alter our regular service," Wayland said.

"But wouldn't it be better?" Alex asked. "The more people we gather, the whole congregation, and in the church, might make praying more productive."

Alex Bradner was playing divine odds. Four was better than two, a crowd more powerful than an individual. Wayland hoped he didn't sound peevish.

"God hears each of us," he said. "Efficacy doesn't require massing."

"I believe in covering all the bases," Alex said.

"God knows our needs," Wayland explained. "He meets them out of His love for us. We don't pray to ask favors as if He's a rich uncle, but to have fellowship with Him, to achieve a feeling that we are close and in His care."

"Would it hurt to try?" Alex asked, pragmatic and relentless.

"I don't suppose it could hurt anything," Wayland said. "The question is whether or not our regular worship service ought to be used. I don't object to rain as part of the general prayer, but to make rain the point of an entire service not only might set a precedent whereby people would soon request snow on Christmas or cooling breezes in August, but would also presume on God's plans for us in this world. Loving and seeking Him is the great prayer, and He will order affairs so that we want nothing in any essential way."

"You won't do it, then?" Alex asked, and tightened his broad, ruddy hands on the aluminum chair arms to stand.

"I'm not speaking that strongly," Wayland said. "As I pray for the sick and the lost, I'll pray for rain, but not use the entire service."

"A lot of people are going to be out of work," Alex said.

•

Alex' visit soured the day for Wayland. He capped his paints, cleaned his brushes, and talked with Mims in the kitchen. She was thirty-three, four years younger than he, a small, neat woman with brown eyes and hair.

"But what can Mr. Wheeler-Dealer do?" she asked. She smelled of vinegar and linseed oil from working at refinishing a pine washstand she had bought at a farm auction.

"I don't know, but I can tell you Alex won't let go," Wayland said.

On Tuesday night, as Wayland was about to close the deacons' meeting with a prayer, Harlan Henderson spoke. Harlan chaired the group, a weathered, square-jawed man who was the county agent.

"Are you going to take any action on the rain?" Harlan asked.

"You mean me personally?" Wayland asked, and got a laugh.

"There's sentiment among the congregation for a special day," Harlan persisted.

"I've winded that sentiment," Wayland said. "I have to tell you frankly I don't like the idea."

"We could sure God use a rain," Nelson Dunnavant said. Nelson had only one arm. He had lost the other to the claws of a mechanical corn picker. He owned both a dairy farm and a John Deere dealership.

"I want rain as much as anyone, but my feeling is rain is a lesser need," Wayland said. "If we're going to unite our voices, we should ask for grateful hearts, not put in a special order. I hope you see the distinction."

He looked into their faces, good faces, of good men, his friends and helpers, men he loved and could rely on, but he observed that they did not see any distinction. They reminded him of cattle staring motionless in a pasture.

"I suggest some things have to be left to the minister's best judgment," Wayland said.

As he walked home through the dry, abrasive darkness, he slapped at mosquitoes, which despite the drought continued to breed along the diminishing river. Seared grass crackled under his shoes. Mims sat in the manse parlor playing the black upright piano. Barefoot, wearing white shorts and a yellow halter, she was practicing hymns to be sung at Sunday School.

"You heard a weather report?" he asked.

"Rain?" she asked, brightening. Her fingers stilled on the keys.

"I was hoping you'd listened and could tell me," he said.

"Sorry there, fellow. Failed once again by your trifling, weakminded wife."

He laughed, crossed to sit by her on the piano bench, and kissed her shoulder, neck, ear, and mouth. She wore perfume, but he still smelled the vinegar.

"Keep this up and you'll have to race me to the bedroom," she said.

When, on Wednesday morning, he walked to the post office, heat quivered above the gummy asphalt street. Lawns were a pale, kinky brown, scorched right to the soil. The soil itself had cracked as if the earth would give up its dead. No flowers bloomed, no sprinklers spun.

Beyond the iron bridge over the shallow, dust-filmed river, cars were leaving the fenced parking lot at the mill. He first thought 10:40 was a strange time for a shift change. Then he understood the men had been let go.

As he walked through the listless, sun-dazzled town, he had a sense that people were eyeing him. He might be imagining it. Ministers developed persecution feelings. The most intent eyes could be his own, peering at himself from within.

"Hear about the plant closing?" Spud Hogge, cashier and a member of the congregation, asked when Wayland stopped by the Planters & Merchants Bank to deposit his bimonthly salary check.

"Terrible for the men," Wayland said. Was he being criticized?

"Rough to have no beans for your family," Spud said, his lumpy face set. When the bell mechanism had broken in the church steeple, Spud had climbed through cobwebs and among rafters. In order to find the trouble and fix it, he'd endured being stung by wasps.

"Spud, are you sending me a message?" Wayland asked, smiling.

"I think everybody has a Christian duty to help all he can in tight times," Spud said, his chin raised as if he intended to push forward with it.

Wayland walked home, changed into shorts, and sat in his study. He would preach this Sunday on the sacrament of baptism. Obviously too he needed to work up a sermon on prayer, its nature.

Despite the open windows, no air moved in his study. It wasn't air at all but a tormenting pressure that galled the skin. The mimosa, stirred by even the slightest breeze, was immobile against a citrine sky, its dusty, drooping fronds tinged yellow. No bird flew, no cloud floated. It would not rain today.

In this week's sermon he meant to emphasize that a man's being immersed symbolized drowning and the death of an old life, and the emergence of a new person into a new life. It occurred to him that the subject of baptism might cause the congregation to think all the more about water and drought. He imagined some wag remarking that there wasn't enough river left to baptize even a dainty Episcopalian.

He was conscious of the weltering locusts, their chirring warping over the parched town. He scratched his bare stomach. He switched on a radio that sat in his bookshelf. The Town Council was asking citizens to take as few baths as possible. His routine called for two showers a day. He considered which to deny himself.

He wrote pell-mell, having no thought for jarring transitions or even scriptural relevance but just trying to get something on paper to work with. Afterwards it would be polish, polish, polish till Saturday, when he would tape the sermon in order that he and Mims could listen and judge how it'd play in Peoria.

The ladies arrived at four and rang the bell—Bess Blakley, Ellen Bowser, and Caroline Devereaux, each a Women of the Church officer. Mims seated them in the parlor and came for Wayland. She rolled her eyes.

There was no way he could slip past them and up the steps to change into proper clothes without being seen. He did hurriedly pull on his red tanktop and apologize for his shoeless feet. Caroline Devereaux looked at his hairy legs. Aware of his bare skin and the ladies' finery, he sat on a leatherette ottoman.

"We're a delegation," Bess Blakley said. Oldest of the three, she had wispy, bluish white hair. "The Women of the Church have gone on record as being in favor of a Special Prayer Day for Rain to end the drought."

Wayland almost sighed openly. The ladies were nearly always the problem. He loved, indeed honored them for being the most devout laborers in Christ's vineyard, but they also became too easily aroused and were regimental in their causes.

"Bess, to repeat my position, let me state that I'm strongly in favor of prayer, but what I feel people really want in this thing is a medicine man, and I never rattle bones, do rain dances, or wear chicken feathers."

"All people want is for you to try," Caroline Devereaux said. She was a tanned, athletic blonde who annually won the town tennis tournament. She also jogged to the river and back every morning, even in winter.

"Caroline, we can't twist God's arm," he explained. "All we have is given us by His grace, and we are undeserving of that."

"We could fill the church," said Ellen Bowser, the wife of Jamerson Bowser, the mayor, who was also in the tobacco export business. Ellen was tiny, hardly five feet tall, yet had mothered six rowdy, robust children.

"Well I'm sure we could, but the service would be a sideshow," Wayland said. "We might also serve popcorn and play bingo."

His sarcasm offended them. They had come to him with serious spiritual business, even if misguided, and he should have been patient and loving.

"It doesn't have to be a sideshow," Bess Blakley said. "I don't see why you and all of us couldn't pray with dignity."

"You're right, Bess, and I'm sorry," he said. "What I'm trying to tell you is, we can't force God's hand even with our most fervent prayers. In praying we shouldn't be talking at all, making demands, but listening, feeling, and receiving Him."

"Then you won't," Caroline Devereaux said. "We heard you were against it."

"Against it, not you," he said. "Refusing you ladies anything distresses me. I'd rather suffer toads and boils. Yet I know you wouldn't want me to do something I consider wrong for myself and our church."

They fidgeted, glanced at each other, and drew their pocketbooks higher on their laps. He walked them to the door, where Ellen Bowser turned to him.

"I hear cattle lowing," she said tearfully. "They sound hurt and mournful. They have no pasture or water. They stand by dry holes looking pitiful. I'd think a minister would be touched by that."

"Believe me, Ellen, I'm not in favor of pain and suffering," Wayland said, and for a moment felt very near despair at the gap between himself and the women, their lives on one side of the theological divide, his life on the other, and so little possibility of ever reaching across and joining hands.

When they were gone, he walked musing to his study. He sat discouraged and began to pray. Depression, rooted in self-pity, he considered a sin. To the Lord he gave thanks for tribulation, as the Epistle of James suggested. All things truly worked for good to those who loved God. And Wayland did love God. When he lifted his head, Mims, hands folded, waited beyond the doorway.

"There wasn't time to warn you," she said. "I had to invite them in."

"It's okay," he said. "I'll be all right now. At least I hope I will."

"You'll feel better after your shower," she said.

"I'm not showering this afternoon," he said.

That night he had a telephone call from Henry Porter of the Danville *Bee*. Henry was nearly inactive in the church, a Christmas Christian.

"Richmond rang my bell," Henry said. "They want a story about this Special Prayer Day for Rain."

"Wait a second," Wayland said. "How would anybody in Richmond know?"

"Can't answer that," Henry said. "I can tell you they might send a reporter. You want to make a statement?"

"I'm definitely holding no Special Prayer Day for Rain," Wayland said. "I'm offering my regular Sunday service, though I will ask for rain in my pastoral prayer."

•

Wayland had trouble sleeping. He worried, and the heat chafed him. Locusts didn't cease their chirring till after eleven o'clock. Then dogs started a monotonous, unrelieved barking. He attempted to lie still so as not to disturb Mims, but he sensed she wasn't sleeping either.

Finally, when he'd nearly dropped off, the telephone rang. He snatched it from the night table.

" 'O ye of little faith!' " a male voice said.

"What?" Wayland asked. "Who is this?"

But the person hung up. Wayland looked at Mims, who lay uncovered in the pearly glow from the bathroom night-light. Her eyes were open.

"I heard it," she said.

"Who'd do that to me?" Wayland asked. He lay beside her and held her moist hand.

"So many people have become irritable in this weather," she said. "Or the call could've come from a tavern."

He was up early Thursday to work on his sermon during the slight morning coolness. There was no dampness on the withered grass. He stayed at his desk until ten. He then drove his Dodge to the community hospital, a modern brick-and-glass structure built on the town's only rise of ground. Stone visitors' benches were placed under shriveled locust and willow trees.

As he made his rounds to the sick and suffering, a voice calling his name echoed along the waxed, metallic corridor. The voice belonged to Lee Gordon, a young doctor whom Wayland had spoken the marriage vows over this past April.

"Margo tells me the phone lines are smoking," Lee said. Margo was his sultry Georgia wife. Lee laughed. "She tells me you're expected to perform miracles."

Trim and virile, Lee, who'd played for the Duke team, was a prowling shark on the golf course. He wore a starched white smock, wine slacks, and perforated black-and-white shoes with kilties. His good-humored assumption that he and Wayland were far more sophisticated about God and religion than anybody else in town disturbed Wayland.

"Miracles happen," Wayland said. "Even today they can." He did believe that, didn't he?

"But you wouldn't want to put your chips on the line, would you?" Lee asked, his teeth gritted in a grin. "I mean right up there in front of everybody in church, to put your chips on the line for a miracle?"

How to make Lee and everyone else understand it wasn't a question of chips on the line? God in His omnipotence could change the course of history by merely willing it, but the question was whether or not God was careless and ran the universe by whim and the seat of His divine trousers.

"Maybe you ought to break over and have a beer," Mims said that afternoon when Wayland, dejected, slumped in his study. She kept a few cans for him. Buying it was dangerous, never done locally, but only while she shopped in Danville or South Hill.

•

The telephone call came at ten minutes after five, not anonymous, but from Fred Pepper, chairman of the Board of Elders. They were scheduling a meeting. Wayland had drunk two beers and was relaxed. He was forced to hurry his eating of Mims's cool shrimp salad and follow it with a slug of Listerine. He fought anger.

There were five elders, veteran Christians, important to the church and to the community. Fred Pepper owned a department store, yet was a man of the cross, always willing to attend presbytery and quick to reach for the check.

"We've been receiving calls," Fred said. He and the other elders sat on the same folding wooden chairs the diaconate used, chairs in a Sunday School room decorated with childish crayon drawings and having a view of the thirsting cemetery. Fred wore a seersucker suit, a white shirt, and a narrow black tie. His gray hair had deep comb furrows in it.

"The ladies are in an uproar," Chap Bonney said. Chap, at least a hundred pounds overweight, was an attorney and on the board at the bank. "Do anything, face storms and earthquakes, lions and tigers, but not the fury of the aroused human female."

Wayland laughed with the others.

"Just what is the problem?" Reid Poindexter asked, precise, mathematical Reid, a dispatcher for the Norfolk Southern Railroad.

"The problem with rain is I'm in sales, not management," Wayland said.

That too got a laugh, though he still had to go through his explanation for refusing to hold the Special Prayer Day for Rain. He had given his reasons so many times he felt he was becoming practiced, smooth, like a sermon repeated till it possessed a singsong momentum of its own.

"It's God's world to do with what He will, and it falls to us to glorify His use of it," Wayland said.

"I thought the world belonged to Satan," Gaston Fervier said. Gaston was a tobacco planter and even now tightened his lip over a dip of snuff, though washed and handsome with his thick white hair, pale blue Palm Beach suit, and polished black shoes. If there was elder trouble, it usually came from Gaston, not because he intended to start it or was mischievous, but because Gaston had his own peculiar manner of seeing everything, including Scriptures.

"God created the world good," Wayland said. "When man sinned through pride, the world was wounded and broken, just as man himself, Adam, was wounded and broken in his relationship to God. In the end, however, all things are still God's."

Gaston stared, his long face not hostile but serious, a trader calculating percentages.

"Maybe it's His will to have us meeting here tonight," Gaston said. "Maybe it's part of His plan to make us hold a Special Prayer Day for Rain."

"Suppose it's not God's purpose to have rain at this time for reasons we can't fathom?" Wayland said, seeing before them the endless convolutions of predestination, which Gaston loved. "Then it won't rain no matter how hard we pray. We'll have held the church and ourselves up to ridicule."

They were silent. When one spoke, it was Carson Puckett, a former superintendent of schools, now in his late seventies, bald, wasting, a deliberate, pious man, pious in the best sense of that misused word.

"Are we afraid to put our faith to the test?" Carson asked. "I believe the Lord will give us rain if we ask for it. He'll find a way."

Wayland hadn't expected it from Carson, a person he greatly respected. He knew the depth of Carson's spirituality. Carson was an Old Testament figure, a patriarch who could strike a rock for water, tread unravished among beasts, and stand unsinged in the fiery furnace. For the first time Wayland felt unsure, even shaken.

"And if we fail?" Wayland asked Carson.

"Then it's us, not God, who've failed," Carson said. "I think it ought to be tried, Pastor. I wish you'd at least consider it."

"I'll of course do that," Wayland said.

Walking home, he felt light-headed. Mims sat fanning herself on the screened porch. In the refrigerator was a glass of iced tea she'd fixed for him.

"Maybe I'm wrong," Wayland said. "I could be behaving like one of these slick modern ministers who act as if Scriptures were private property. I've become so professional I've lost sight of the power of simple belief."

•

Early in the morning he drove to Richmond to see Dr. Hans Koppman, his friend and former teacher, at Union Theological. Dr. Koppman was a brusque and powerful man, one who, unlike many lecturers at the seminary, heaped work on his students because he believed the ministry was life's highest calling and more should be expected of those who aspired to it. He stormed around his classroom demanding answers to questions that were snares. He loved parable and paradox.

Dr. Koppman waited in his office. From his ponderous head his graying black hair grew into tangled ovals, and more hair curled from his porous nose. He whooped, laughed loudly, and repeatedly slapped his desk.

"Oh, brother, I'm glad it's you, not me!" he shouted. "I'd rather be roasted over hot coals. Lord, deliver my heifers from the drought!"

"It's not funny to me," Wayland said.

"So you've come to a foolish professor in a preacher factory and want him to tell you what to do," Dr. Koppman said. "Listen, the understanding of faith is not in the seminaries. Faith exists in the recesses of that mad place, the heart, and who knows the labyrinthine corridors of the heart?"

As Dr. Koppman discoursed, Wayland gazed out the ivy-twined window at tennis players, at the nets and lines on the green courts, at the patterns of white and green, the perfect little world of games. He longed for the certainty of rules.

"I'm reminded of the story about a holy young man who doubted the strength of his belief," Dr. Koppman said. "The young man thought that if he were really strong in the faith, he could walk on water. He traveled to the land's edge. Trembling, he set foot on the stormy depths. Lo, the waters held him! Joy welled in him as he walked over the thrashing waves like a tottering child, glorious, mind-blowing joy. He was fired by the ecstasy of knowing he was favored by God."

"Is that all the story?" Wayland asked.

"Not quite," Dr. Koppman said, his thick brows humping. "In running for joy, he crossed a highway without due care, heard the blast of an air horn, looked up, and saw a bread truck that rolled over and killed him. His last vision was one of loaves."

Dr. Koppman beat the desk and laughed and laughed. Wayland drove home more muddled than ever. He sat in his study and stared at the yellowing mimosa and his desiccated rock garden. He slipped to his knees, rested his elbows on the swivel chair, and raised his face.

"Father, open me to Thy will so that whatever I do may be for Thy glory," he prayed.

Again he gave up his evening shower. After dinner he was unable to stop himself from studying the weather map in the Danville *Bee*. There was no mention of rain across the entire nation.

He returned to his study to work on the baptism sermon. Words wouldn't flow. He watched twilight settle like a sheer gray fabric over the dusty yard. He became fearful. Suppose his indecision indicated some moral chink in his theological armor?

Scratching his hot skin, he roamed the manse. In the kitchen Mims was pinching her rings from the windowsill where she always set them while washing dishes.

"I feel everybody in the country's taking a bite out of me," Wayland said.

"On suffocating days like these, people aren't themselves," she said.

"Who are they?" he asked. He saw she was tired—more than tired, worn.

"We can't expect them to be more than human," she said. Sweaty, wilted, carrying his worries as well as her own, she touched her forehead with the limp back of a hand. It was a beautiful gesture: patient, feminine, long-suffering. And then she served up a smile to encourage him.

He was so moved he could only nod. Oh, he loved her! And her words, such simple ordinary words, but there it was, the whole truth of prayer really, stripped of theology and man's encrustments. To plead when troubled, to go to one's father, was human. God knew our needs, sure, but He wouldn't expect anyone, not even a minister, to be more than human—just as no father would expect a son or daughter to be other than a child.

For an instant Wayland was tormented he hadn't seen the truth, yet grateful he saw it now.

"Would you consider your husband a weak, spineless creature if he reversed himself and decided to hold a rain service?" he asked.

"I'd be so glad!" she said, clasping her hands.

"You would?" he asked. He'd believed she wholly supported his ideas on prayer.

"My husband, the good shepherd, wants to feed his flock," she said.

So Saturday he worked late writing and mimeographing a service for the Special Prayer Day, and on Sunday morning the church was full even to the balconies. Wayland had composed a responsive liturgy in order that the congregation might have a role. He spoke his part over the reverent, upturned faces in the nave—the word *nave* having the same Latin derivation as the word *navy*, and it was as if they were on a ship looking up to him the captain.

"As Your children we humbly come to ask of You," he intoned.

"Lord, bring us rain," the congregation responded.

After the service Wayland's fingers became sore from shaking hands. Men pawed his shoulders. The ladies were gracious, and he and Mims received seven invitations to dinner. Only Gaston Fervier annoyed him.

"I see you didn't bring your umbrella," Gaston said. Gaston had his.

At the manse Mims fixed Wayland a sandwich. She was happy about the service, but he felt emptied. He lay down for a nap.

He would not anticipate. Rain wasn't necessary. He and the congregation had acknowledged God's fathership, which was the main thing. He turned his back to the window so he wouldn't be tempted to judge the quality of the afternoon sunlight edging the drawn blind.

He felt a stillness, the absolute hush of the day. Even the locusts were silent. A distant rumble had to be a truck or plane. He stood, went downstairs, and walked out onto the screened porch where Mims sat. She wore her lavender church dress in case of visitors but had pushed off her white pumps so that her heels were free.

The expression on her shiny face was strange as she gazed upward.

He looked at the sky and, tingling, saw the radiant cloud growing, building rapidly into a thunderhead, the underside purplish, the crown of brilliant whiteness seething as it mounted into a dazzling cathedral of a cloud. People came from their houses to stare. Then Wayland felt a coolness, a nudge of air, and knew rain must be close.

In wonder he and Mims watched the sky. His amazement gave way to rapture as the majestic thunderhead conquered the heavens. He realized his mouth had opened to catch the rain on his lips. The pressure of gratitude brought him near to weeping.

During the slashing, luminous storm, he put on shorts to walk in the yard. With face uplifted, he gave thanks. Children, despite lightning, ran in the streets and across glistening lawns. Adults too hollered and splashed through puddles. The artificial pond in his rock garden overflowed. The telephone rang so often that Mims, now wearing her pink bathing suit, took it off the hook.

Only later, during the wet night when he and Mims lay together, did he think of the holy young man who had walked on water. The story was surely just another of Dr. Koppman's pranks, but the truth is that for days Wayland not only looked in both directions with extreme care before crossing streets, even the least traveled ones, but also peered at ceilings, floors, the ground, tree limbs, and into shadows, as if something waited for him.